Holden staggered to his knees, half fell, mule-kicking the man in the face with his left foot.

The .45—the FLNAer was going for it. Holden's fist closed on the butt of the Beretta Compact and he ripped it from the leather holster.

The water beside his head exploded as the FLNAer's .45 discharged. Holden punched the 9mm forward and fired twice, then twice again, then twice more, the FLNAer's neck and face splotching red, the eyes rolling wide, the .45 falling from his fist as it opened, the body toppling back. Holden fired twice more; the body twitched as it fell down.

Holden rolled over into the water. He pushed himself back to his knees.

Men stared down from the overlook of the ravine.

Holden waited for the gunfire to start. . . .

# OUT
## OF
# CONTROL

## Jerry Ahern

A DELL BOOK

Published by
Dell Publishing
a division of
The Bantam Doubleday Dell
Publishing Group, Inc.
666 Fifth Avenue
New York, New York 10103

ISBN: 0-440-20101-2

Printed in the United States of America

Published simultaneously in Canada

November 1988

10 9 8 7 6 5 4 3 2 1

KRI

*For all the people who don't just let somebody else vote—*
*you are the Heroes who make Freedom work!*

# CHAPTER

# 1

Crouching low as he ran, David Holden moved along the ridgeline, the M-16's pistol grip vised in his black-gloved right fist. His eyes narrowed involuntarily against the brightness of the postdawn sunrise, which winked unexpectedly from beneath the heavy gray overcast. His combat boots made squishing and slapping sounds as they suctioned in and out of the mud. The footing was poor, but he moved as quickly as he could.

Below Holden, on the two-lane U.S. highway, the imported pickup truck with the flashing orange emergency lights and the sign reading WIDE LOAD moved very slowly, obviously to avoid outdistancing the full-size truck cab which towed the cedar-sided mobile home upward along the winding roadway deeper into the mountains. Behind it was a mid-size American car, the car outfitted identically with blinking orange flashers and a wide-load sign.

Holden found the terrain features he had memorized by flashlight in the predawn darkness and started down from the ridgeline, along a mud- and gravel-strewn defile between patches of wild blackberry vines and partially uprooted scrub pines.

The morning was already warm, and the small of Holden's back underneath his black BDUs felt wet with sweat. His pace slowed from the run to a cautious, skidding commando walk as he picked his way downward.

The terrain opening suddenly before him was, under any circumstances, beautiful, and had there been time to ponder the ranks of upthrusting peaks and neatly farmed valleys, mists lingering across them against the advancing daylight like a lover's last kiss of morning, David Holden would have considered it poetically inspiring.

But there had been little time for inspiration since the Front for the Liberation of North America had begun its "people's revolution" of terror—how long ago? And the only poetry had been death. Like many men, when he had been young, he had written ardent and dubiously artistic poems to his wife, which she had folded away in the bottom of a drawer somewhere and mercifully never shown to anyone else. But she was dead, his son and two daughters dead as well, all casualties in this insanity of revolution.

The police and the military were on one side, the FLNA killers on the other, the American people trapped in the violent middle. And out of the American people had risen the Patriots.

David Holden kept moving and reached the trailing edge of the defile, the convoy momentarily out of view as he worked his way left into a natural rock battlement selected days earlier, when the Patriots had first learned the Front for the Liberation of North America would be moving its cargo along this normally quiet mountain road.

"David!" Rosie Shepherd's voice whispered from beyond the rocks. He clambered up over them and dropped down beside Rosie and the six other Patriot cell members with her. "Everything—"

"Everything's set. Patsy and the others are in that ditch by the side of the road—down there." He gestured toward the far side shoulder.

"Lucky them." She smiled. Her green eyes were pretty when she smiled. It was odd, when she slept and, sometimes, he could not, and it was light enough to clearly see her face, with her eyes closed, the lids were like theater curtains awaiting the beginning of some great and wonderful show—when her eyes would open.

Holden looked away from her, watching the road as the convoy wound along it toward them. The tip had come from an increasingly good source of intelligence data concerning FLNA activities from the wife of a reporter named Evans who worked hand in glove with the FLNA's overall field commander in the area surrounding Metro and the city itself. They knew nothing about the field commander except his name, which was likely an alias. The name was Johnson. But in the weeks since the aborted attempt by the FLNA to assassinate the director of the Federal Bureau of Investigation and implicate the Patriots, Holden had become increasingly more wary. It was known that the FBI had assigned a special team to penetrate the Patriots. The reason seemed obvious. Although the Patriots did a job no police or military unit seemed able to do—brought the war to the FLNA and inflicted heavy damage and heavy casualties—they, it seemed, were a greater thorn in the side of government than the FLNA revolutionaries were. And the desire of police and military forces to eradicate the Patriots seemed stronger than any desire to eradicate the FLNA.

The Patriots were outlaws, even more condemned in

the liberal-biased press and media than the FLNA, despite the FLNA's bombing of churches and synagogues and universities and public buildings and police stations and places where the military congregated in off-duty hours, despite the power blackouts from transformer topplings that were so regular an event they were sometimes barely noticed, despite the inexorably collapsing economy. Because factories and warehouses were firebombed, workers were too terrified to come to work even in daylight, while night shifts were all but a thing of the past in some areas.

Patsy Alfredi's people would close on the convoy from its left flank. Holden watched along the ditch now, seeing no sign of their presence. And that was good. Patsy Alfredi's husband had been a cop, been killed by the FLNA. Death here was a common bond.

He heard the sounds of some of the Patriots around him making last-minute weapons checks. Holden looked back at Rosie. She knelt in the grass there behind the rocks in perfect calm, her M-16 lying across her lap the way some women might rest their needlework.

Holden made a last-minute equipment check. The Bianchi flap holster beside his left hipbone with the full-size Beretta 92-F 9mm was secure; the shoulder rig with the 92-F Compact, the two twenty-round extension magazines, and the inverted sheath with the Crain Defender knife were as they should be. On his right thigh was the Southwind Sanctions SAS-style holster with the Desert Eagle .44 Magnum.

He thought about the gun. Holden had taken the Desert Eagle from Rufus Burroughs's dead body. Burroughs was the man who had gotten the Patriots in Metro going, the police officer whose wife had been one of the earliest Patriot victims, the man who had himself rescued Holden from false imprisonment and brought him into the Patriots, the man who had given his life during the battle to prevent the FLNA from precipitating a disastrous meltdown of the Plant Wright nuclear reactor's core.

The gun was a tangible symbol to Holden of the promise he had never made Burroughs in life: that someday the FLNA would be crushed and America would be safe once again.

Holden touched the butt of the pistol with his fingertips, then looked down along the road again. The convoy was nearly into position. "Be ready," he cautioned.

There was the rattle of a sling that shouldn't have rattled, the creaking of a leather holster, the scratch of metal against fabric, a cough.

The convoy rounded a tight hairpin bend in the road, slowing because of the steep upward angle and the angle of the curve itself.

The imported pickup passed Patsy Alfredi's position. Then the semi hauling the mobile home blotted her position from view.

Gunfire blasted from beside the road, and the trailing vehicle in the convoy—the mid-size American car— veered to the right, across the near shoulder, the windshield shot out. A grenade was hurled, rolled across the roadbed, and stopped beneath the mid-size car. There was a dull roar and then an earsplittingly loud crack. The car was consumed with flames.

A living torch stumbled from the driver's seat as Holden shouted to Rosie and the others, "Let's go!" The living torch fell and crawled across the highway. Gunfire from Patsy Alfredi's people ripped across the tarmac, ending the driver's agony.

Holden ran, half skidded, jumped a deadfall tree and a clump of high brush near it, reached the road shoulder, running full out now, Rosie almost but not quite beside him. Since recovering from the head wound he had sustained aboard the train when he and Rosie had foiled the assassination plot against Rudolph Cerillia, the FBI director, Holden had begun to use his few free hours training. And the training was paying off, the softness of his life as a history professor at Thomas Jefferson University fading from him. He ran into the center of the roadway now, shouting to the others, "Open fire!"

Holden's M-16 bucked in his hands as he blew the entire magazine into the radiator of the imported pickup. Automatic-weapons fire from the pickup's cab came back at him. There was a rumbling sound, and the pickup's hood blew upward and open. The pickup angled across the road toward the edge and the drop beyond. The driver jumped clear, rolling across the pavement. The figure in the passenger seat kept firing as the truck drew near the edge.

The door swung open, and the gunman jumped clear, came down hard, rolled, went into a prone position, and was still firing as the pickup suddenly went airborne over the side of the road, then dropped like a carelessly tossed stone.

Heavy automatic-weapons fire was coming from the mobile home toward both sides of the roadbed. It was supposed to be carrying cargo, not FLNAers.

Holden reloaded his assault rifle and turned the muzzle toward the gunman, firing three-round bursts as he charged toward him, with Rosie and two of the others flanking him. The gunman's body was taking hit after hit, vibrating with the impacts. The weapon—an Uzi submachine gun—fell from his hands to the road surface as his body rocked back and was still.

The semi with the mobile home— "Look out!" Holden

grabbed at Rosie Shepherd's BDU collar and dragged her out of its way, almost pulling her off her feet.

As he let go of her, he stuffed his safed M-16 into Rosie's hands and ran. Something had gone wrong.

Holden was now alongside the cedar-sided mobile home. Gunfire was coming from its windows, but the shooters were still firing into both roadbeds. Holden kept low, running under their fire until he reached the door.

Holden jumped and grabbed the door handle with his right hand. His left hand went to his web gear, reaching toward the three grenades there. Holden ripped one free of its pin. High-explosive. His left arm arced out, and he hurtled the grenade in through one of the open windows through which the FLNA riflemen had fired. Then Holden jumped clear, hitting the road surface in a roll, his left shoulder taking most of the impact. "Dammit!" Holden growled. But he got up running, his right hand to his left shoulder as the explosion came, a two-stage roar, first dull, then loud.

There had been explosives or gasoline aboard, Holden realized, something his grenade had activated.

He stopped running, and backstepped, raising his right hand and forearm to protect his face and eyes. A fireball, black and orange, belched skyward, flames licking outward from beneath the mobile home's frame as first the mobile home, then the truck cab, began upending. The mobile home became a hard-edged elongated sphere of flame, twisting the cab after it in a roll, toward the edge of the roadway where the pickup had disappeared.

Holden lowered his arm; his hand rested on the butt of the Desert Eagle .44.

A body jumped clear of the truck cab, the man falling to his knees, a Mini-Uzi stabbing outward in his right hand. Holden's own right hand moved, popping the safety strap on the Southwind Sanctions holster, tearing the Desert Eagle free. His thumb jacked back the hammer. As the Desert Eagle bucked in his fist, there was a burst of automatic-weapons fire from his left. The Mini-Uzi discharged, the tarmac near his feet rippling with the bullets. Visible at the far lower edge of his line of sight as he shot again was the Desert Eagle at full extension of his right arm.

The FLNAer's body was already twisting, flopped back, down, the little submachine gun discharging into the air, then tumbling from dead fingers.

Holden wheeled left, toward the source of the automatic-weapons fire. "You're gettin' pretty good with that, Tex." Rosie Shepherd grinned, an M-16 in a hard assault position beside her right hip.

Holden had found a ready supply of .44 Magnum cartridges and, as with his running and lifting, had practiced with the Desert Eagle.

As he walked toward the dead man, he was glad that he had.

# CHAPTER

## 2

Dimitri Borsoi poured a glass of sherry from the de-
canter and sipped at it as he looked over the rim of the
glass, inspecting his surroundings. He only half listened
as Humphrey Hodges spoke, but that was all that was
usually necessary. "This election is vital, Mr. Johnson. I
don't know what your instructions are concerning it,
but—"

"Let me tell you," Borsoi began, "what my instructions are, Professor Hodges." He liked the French Im-
pressionist paintings—obvious copies—which were
neatly arranged on the far wall beneath individual brass
fluorescent fixtures. He turned his eyes toward the lock-
fitted glass-front bookcase and the collection of what appeared to be first editions, not copies. "Elections are taking place all over this country. But our concern here this
evening is Metro. The mayoral race. Roger Costigan is
basing his campaign on the FLNA question. If the ideas
Costigan is putting forth became the reality of an administrative program in Metro, FLNA activities would be
severely hampered. It is our mission to disrupt the Costigan campaign at all costs—"

"Why not—" Hodges interrupted.

"Assassinate him?" Borsoi in turn interrupted. He limped slightly as he walked, a reminder of the injury sustained to his right leg during the FBI shoot-out weeks ago before the unsuccessful attempt to assassinate Rudolph Cerillia. He told himself that if he had been physically able, things would have ended differently. And that paid assassin they had hired, who called himself Warlock. The man's much-vaunted talents had proved totally useless against even a talented amateur like this David Holden. "Assassination? No. We want the people of Metro to stay away from the polls. We want those who do risk their lives to vote to be doing that literally. Polling places will be hit, ballots stolen or burned, voters killed. And before the election, political rallies, everything related to the campaign that can be disrupted will be disrupted, and as violently as possible. Let the American people see what elections are like in other parts of their so-called free world."

"Then Harris Ganby is the man we're supporting—"

Borsoi laughed as he sat down opposite Hodges's desk, set down his glass of sherry, and lit a cigarette. "Harris Ganby's candidacy is not our concern. But Roger Costigan's law-and-order program is our target."

"But what if Costigan wins anyway?"

Dimitri Borsoi found Humphrey Hodges so wonderfully obtuse that it was sometimes hard to imagine the man being able to deduce the sum of two and two without a calculator.

# CHAPTER
# 3

Luther Steel faced a man in a business suit shielded by a frightened female hostage, and in the man's hand was a gaping muzzled revolver.

Steel drew the Sig-Sauer P-226 from beneath the jacket of his khaki summer suit. He set it on the small Formica-covered table in front of him.

He took a deep breath, then picked up the 9mm pistol, holding it low. He snapped it up into a point-shoulder position, the rear sight rising first, the front sight rising into it as his right first finger snapped back, so infinitesimally slight a delay between the first and second shot that only he was aware of it, another double tap, then another.

Steel lowered the pistol as he worked the decocking lever, then shifted the pistol into his left hand to activate the return button. He had once known a police officer who had been involved in the local end of a federal case. The man had, a year later, died in a gunfight. He had shot his opponent, cleared the cylinder of his revolver, and, after speed-loading, bent over to pick up his spent brass, a habit he had picked up firing on the range.

For that reason Luther Steel never formed range hab-
its, and for that reason he usually shot alone. The correct
thing to have done would have been to set down his pistol
after removing the magazine and clearing the chamber,
then to have let the slide remain locked open. But if, in
the heat of battle, he were to do that, he would die. This
warfare with the FLNA had caused the deaths of three
bureau men already. He had no desire to be the fourth or
some subsequent number.

The target returned, and he had, neatly, put a trail of
six shots leading vertically into it. The group started in
the offender's throat, and the last bullet penetrated at the
bridge of the nose. Shooting these days, he reflected, was
more serious a business than it had ever been.

For the effective use of a firearm in the hands of a law-
enforcement professional, ultimate accuracy was required
during practice because in the stress of real-life combat,
performance efficiency would be drastically reduced.
Heart and respiration rates were accelerated, the hand
shook, and whatever could possibly go wrong might and
had to be accounted for.

He ran the target back to seventy-five feet, where it had
been before, and, as he did, opened the green plastic
MTM box and extracted six Federal 115-grain Jacketed
Hollow Points, removed the magazine from the pistol,
replaced the six shots fired, then reinserted the magazine.
If some distraction were to come up and he forgot to
reload, he would have only ten rounds (counting the one
in the chamber) instead of sixteen.

He reholstered the Sig in the Sparks Summer Special
beside his left kidney, then reached under his right armpit to the Bianchi 9R shoulder rig and snapped the 66
2½ from the leather. He never used .357 Magnums in it,
only .38 Special Plus Ps, 158-grain Lead Semi-wadcutter

Hollow Points. Felt recoil in the little stainless K-Frame Smith & Wesson was deleterious to good marksmanship with .357s. Because of the short barrel, the superiority of .357s over .38 Plus Ps was dubious at best, and the shortened ejector rod stroke of the snubby 66 was insufficient to clear the marginally longer .357 brass surely.

The target reached its computer-predesignated stopping point.

Luther Steel punched the 66 out to nearly the full extension of his right arm, fired a double tap, brought his left hand up, shifting his body into a point shoulder, fired another double tap, then shifted the revolver fully into his left hand, double-actioning it twice more.

He kept the revolver in his left hand as he recalled the target. In the many weeks since he had been assigned the job of locating David Holden, leader of the Patriot cell in greater Metro, he had gotten very close. Rudolph Cerillia, the director, had been very patient. Steel had spent one long three-day weekend back with his family in Wisconsin, then made a quick stop in Detroit to fill out a deposition on the kidnap case he'd been working prior to Mr. Cerillia's special assignment, before he was back in Metro.

He had struck up a friendship with another black agent in the Detroit area, who had said to him, "Whatever job the director's got you on, Luther, you may see your kids in time for them to graduate from college if you play it right." Luther Steel hadn't found the thought amusing.

With one of the Safariland speed loaders, he recharged the revolver's cylinder as the target stopped. Six holes, wider apart than with the autoloading 9mm, but satisfactorily tight, lay in two gradually ascending parallel lines along the upper arm and into the right shoulder of the target.

From a second plastic box he replaced the six spent federal .38 Specials and locked the control knob of the speed loader. He dropped the speed loader into his outside jacket pocket.

Each day that circumstances permitted—and that was most days if he managed his time well—Luther Steel fired a minimum of twelve rounds. Each night he carefully inspected both handguns, and at least once each week he cleaned them.

Because of his wife and kids, perhaps, he took his street survival very seriously. There was the FLNA. There was the organization he was trying to penetrate, the Patriots. Crime was rising almost exponentially, violence a daily occurrence on a grander scale than ever before in American history.

Those who didn't take survival on the streets seriously eventually no longer had to concern themselves with it.

He removed his shooter's muffs and his amber-tinted glasses, reholstered the revolver under his arm, then started for the steps leading up from the basement range. He had a group under his direct command. None of them knew the specific purpose of their assignment; only one of them, he thought, suspected.

The one who suspected was the oldest of the group, a man named Clark Pietrowski, who had worked out of the Metro office for fourteen years and knew the city better than most taxicab drivers, knew its crime and the warrens of its criminals better than any city policeman.

As if some sixth sense had warned him, Luther Steel saw Clark Pietrowski at the head of the stairs. "They need ya upstairs, Luther—figured I'd come for ya."

Luther Steel changed his pace to take the stairs three at

a time, following Pietrowski along the corridor. In seconds he was beside him and cut back his stride to avoid passing the older man.

Pietrowski was pushing retirement age, but since the emergency period had begun, agents older than Pietrowski were being retained, usually in administrative capacities. Luther Steel considered Pietrowski an asset. As a field agent. "What's going on, Clark?"

"Damned if I know, Luther. This woman was brought into Metro Central Hospital about forty-five minutes ago. Her name is Harriet Evans. She kept calling for somebody named Holden, and the uniformed cop there put two and two together, slapped her into isolation except for medical personnel, and called in. Could be *the* Holden we're looking for, maybe not. I just got the poop on that through an informant I have in the police department."

"We're federal agents—"

"And we're not supposed to have informants in the police department. I know that."

"So then—"

"No, Luther. I was just on my way when a phone call from Ralph Kaminsky came in. Hadda talk to you. Sounded urgent, so I went to get ya."

Ralph Kaminsky was the deputy commander of Metro PD, bald, skinny, beady-eyed, and nasty-tongued. Steel smiled as he thought of it—those were almost Kaminsky's good points.

Luther Steel turned into his office, Clark Pietrowski falling back. "Come on in, Clark," Steel told the older man.

Anna Comacho, who was filing, looked up from the file cabinet and said, "Deputy Commander Kaminsky's on hold on line three, Mr. Steel."

"Thanks, Anna," he told her, and her dark eyes smiled

back. He went through his open office door, Clark Pietrowski behind him. "Close the door, huh?" He had few secrets from the unit's secretary, but there was no sense broadcasting. Pietrowski set his lean gray frame onto a corner of the desk, lit a cigarette, and put on his glasses. Steel picked up the phone and punched line three. "Deputy Commander Kaminsky? This is Luther Steel. What can I do for you, sir?"

The voice matched Kaminsky's other strong points, raspy and oily at once. "What the fuck are you doing down there?"

"Sir?"

"One of my men just got himself shot down ten minutes ago. Dead. Trying to stop somebody stealing drugs out of an ambulance at Metro Hospital. They found the name of one of your men and two telephone numbers on a card in his breast pocket; one of the phone numbers was your office, and the other I checked out. Belongs to that old fart Clark Pietrowski. What the hell are you doing?"

Steel looked at Pietrowski. He covered the mouthpiece and hissed, "Your guy is dead, Clark."

"Ask the asshole what his alibi was for the time." Pietrowski smiled back.

"What's going on?" Kaminsky's voice crackled through the receiver.

Steel cleared his throat, said, "I have no specific answer for you, Mr. Kaminsky, but Special Agent Pietrowski's well known for his long-standing good relationship with local authorities, and I'd say the most likely explanation for your dead officer's having the office number and Agent Pietrowski's home phone is that they were friends. Why it was in his pocket, who knows? Perhaps he was cleaning out his wallet. There could be a wealth of possible explanations, and with the man deceased, the likelihood of determining the exact reason is remote. Please express my personal condolences to the officer's family. And I'll alert Special Agent Pietrowski to the man's death. He'll ask the name, of course."

There was silence for a minute. Then Kaminsky's voice came back, sounding as if he were reading. "Patrolman Reginald Wendt."

"Patrolman Wendt, you say," Steel repeated, watching Pietrowski's eyes. They went hard, and Pietrowski inhaled on his cigarette, then looked away. "I'll tell Special Agent Pietrowski about this conversation. If he can shed any further light on the circumstances concerning the telephone numbers, I'll be in touch. Thank you for calling this to my attention, Mr. Kaminsky."

The line clicked dead. Steel held the receiver away from his face and looked at it for a few seconds. "Unpleasant man," Steel remarked.

"Shithead's a better term," Pietrowski rasped.

Steel hung up the telephone. "Wendt was your informant?"

"Yeah, Luther. And I betcha that wasn't some druggy snitchin' shit out of some goddamned ambulance who smoked him either."

"And?"

"Luther, you want David Holden. I'm bettin' you want him to talk with, not to bust. And I know you can't tell me what's goin' on 'cause it's between you and Mr. Cerillia. But just in case I'm right, if this woman in the hospital is calling for the Holden that we want, I betcha the FLNA is gonna go after her next."

There was a knock at the door, the door opened, and Anna Comacho came halfway inside. "Clark, I got some background on that Mrs. Harriet Evans. You were right. She is the wife of that TV news guy."

"Bingo!" Clark Pietrowski smiled, uncoiled off the desk, and planted a kiss on Anna Comacho's cheek. He looked at Steel. "Well, boss?"

"I can't kidnap her out of a hospital, but I can guard her. Anna, work up something that sounds official but doesn't say anything about how Mrs. Harriet Evans is a possible federal witness. Find something we can tie her into for a few hours."

"Right, Mr. Steel."

Luther Steel hit the comline button on his phone and dialed Tom LeFleur's desk. "Tom, Luther. Check with Anna. Dig out all the dope you can on a Mrs. Harriet Evans and her husband. Anna's got the poop. Shout over to Bill, and get him into my office. Have Randy help you."

"Right, Luther."

Steel appraised Clark Pietrowski. "Gonna cost me my ass, old man." Steel laughed.

Pietrowski drew his revolver, checked the cylinder, closed it, replaced it in the crossdraw holster. "I've got more pension to lose, Luther." Pietrowski smiled.

There was a knock. Bill Runningdeer stepped half inside. "Luther?"

"Grab us a car. Take your raincoat, and draw an Uzi and three magazines. Downstairs in two minutes."

"You bet." Bill Runningdeer vanished.

"Sounds like it might be fun after all, huh?" Clark Pietrowski grinned.

# CHAPTER
## 4

Dimitri Borsoi turned the key and drove the van away from the curb fronting the red-brick ranch house, giving a glance to his wristwatch. Achmed Ferrazzi, whom the loud-talking boys of the street gangs like the Leopards knew as Abner, was sitting beside him, calmly smoking a cigarette. The boys were telling dirty jokes, which wouldn't have offended Borsoi except for the fact that they were so bad.

"This Evans, he is dangerous."

"He *was* dangerous." Borsoi corrected him. The sweep second hand reached twelve, and there was a sharp cracking sound, followed first by a low rumble then by a roar as he looked into the passenger-side west coast mirror.

The house was in flames, a mushroom-shaped cloud of fire and smoke rising into the hot afternoon air. Now there was only the question of Evans's wife. "What kind of despicable man shoots his wife?" Ferrazzi asked suddenly.

Borsoi only looked at him, half in shock. Achmed Ferrazzi was one of the most wanted men in the Middle East and Europe, and the killings to his record were counted in triple digits at the least. "You're serious?"

"Of course, I am serious—Mr. Johnson," he added for effect.

"He was a valuable man. Cowardly but valuable. And I suppose his cowardice was what drove him to try to kill her. But he couldn't even do that right."

"This is all right. She is being killed for a purpose. He tried to kill her because he could not control her. That is no purpose worthy of a man. A man who cannot control his wife cannot control his urine, either, I think. And then to tell you to finish the job!"

"Thank your god that he did," Borsoi told him, taking the van up onto the feeder ramp, slowing, blending in with the flow of traffic. Sirens in the distance responded to the explosion. A charred body tied into a chair with a bullet in the brain would be all they would find, if any of Evans's body remained at all. "She has been informing on our movements to the Patriots. It is the pity that we must kill her because with a little time she could be made to tell us all she knows concerning David Holden, this Shepherd woman, and the others. But if she should talk, she knows my face. She knows a great deal, I think. Evans spoke with her too much."

"A man should not discuss such matters with women. The Americans are decadent."

"Also poor shots." Borsoi smiled. Evans, according to the FLNA source who had gotten them information concerning Harriet Evans, had only wounded his wife, seriously but not fatally. She had driven herself to the hospital, collapsed in the parking lot, been isolated in intensive care.

"There will be police."

"None of them will be ours," Borsoi said.

"Fine. Then we will kill them all."

"Do you have enough?"

"One whole wing of the hospital will go up. Mrs. Evans will vanish from the face of the earth, and all around her."

"We can turn this to our advantage." Borsoi nodded.

The connector ramp was coming up, and he signaled and moved right a lane. Another glance at his watch. Not too much time remained.

# CHAPTER
# 5

Mitch Diamond had gotten the call, and the powerful base station he used for his flourishing wrecker business had contacted them within, as Diamond put it, "less than a minute."

She was dressing as they drove, and it was evident to her that David Holden had no conception of what it was like to put on pantyhose, or he would have not taken his turns so quickly. She knew the route by heart without having to see it—as she could not do from the inside of the van, the curtains drawn as they were—and she knew each turn. He had just gotten onto the expressway leading into the city. With the false identity papers they could have so easily manufactured now, and with the wonderfully talented Mimi Baker joining their ranks, travel had become much easier.

She stood up when she judged it might be safe to do so for thirty seconds and jumped, tugging at the waistband, finally getting the white pantyhose as they should be. She risked standing long enough to pull on a pair of panties and a slip, both white.

If she had to, she could get into the nurse's uniform

while seated. A sudden turn, and she shouted out, "Dammit, David!"

"Sorry!"

"Next time you try getting dressed up like a nurse in the back of a van, huh!" The thought amused her, and she went back to dressing.

Mitch Diamond had relayed that Harriet Evans, their most valuable contact for information concerning movements and operations of the FLNA, had been shot, was in intensive care and calling for David.

Was this somehow related to the fiasco earlier this day? Patsy Alfredi had nearly been killed, two of the others been wounded, and the FLNA arms David had been looking to expropriate for Patriot use been destroyed.

She was buttoning the front of the dress, her eyes drifting to the Null shoulder holster she usually carried. But she couldn't get into the hospital with it. "Dammit!"

"What's wrong now, Rosie?"

"Nothing. I just thought about walking around without any weapons."

"You find out what you can, talk to Harriet Evans if you can, then get out. If she needs extraction, we'll come back in force," David cautioned her.

Rosie Shepherd knew the drill.

She took up the mirror. Mimi had done a quick job of the makeup, darkening Rosie's complexion, darkening the eyebrows, and, of course, adding the contact lenses. All Rosie had to do was put on the wig.

She put the little cap over her hair, packed her hair up inside it, then took the wig from the small box. Dishwater blond had never been a look she'd wanted to try. Once the wig was in place, she saw why. She pinned the nurse's white cap in place.

"Almost to the hospital, Rosie. Far as I can go is the outer parking lot."

"I'll be all right." She began to tie the white shoes she'd borrowed from a beautician.

# CHAPTER
## 6

Luther Steel, flanked by Clark Pietrowski and Bill Runningdeer, walked across the hospital lobby. The two rental security people he'd expected to find (that was the usual thing at any event) had been replaced by Metro city cops.

Steel took his ID case from his jacket, glanced once at Bill Runningdeer to make certain the submachine gun didn't show under the raincoat the American Indian wore, then quickened his pace.

"I'm Luther Steel, AIC for the special task force. We need access to the eighth floor."

He started past the cops as he pocketed his ID case.

"Sorry, Agent Steel."

Steel stopped in his tracks, turned around, touched at Clark Pietrowski's left forearm to shut him up. "Officer" —Steel looked at the nameplate over the shirt pocket— "Officer Calhoun. This is official government business."

"I have orders, Agent Steel."

Steel studied the man's face for a moment. He didn't like it. The eyes were hiding something, and it was not embarrassment. "What kind of orders? Keep the FBI out?"

"That's it. So—why don't you call downtown, huh?"

"Because a Mrs. Harriet Evans is on the eighth floor in the ICU there?"

"Look, Leroy, just call—"

"It's Luther, Luther Steel. You call me Leroy again and I'll kick your ass."

The cop started to move his right hand. It could have been construed as reaching for a gun, Luther Steel told himself, and Director Cerillia had told him that he'd back him one hundred percent. Steel's left hand moved to block the gun. His right hand bunched into a fist, then crossed the policeman's jaw in a short, tight jab.

The second Metro cop was backing off. Calhoun spilled back into the security desk and skidded to the floor, a dazed look in his eyes.

"You're good, Luther," Clark Pietrowski observed.

"Golden Gloves when I was a kid. Just like tap dancing. We all do it." Steel grinned. Then he looked at the other Metro cop. "You got any problems with these two other agents and myself going upstairs, Officer?"

"I'm to warn you that you are disobeying a police order, sir," the second cop said shakily.

"I shall consider myself duly warned. Take care of your friend. A plastic bag with some ice should be obtainable at the coffee shop." Luther Steel turned and walked away. Bill Runningdeer was laughing. Clark Pietrowski pushed the elevator call button. The doors opened, they stepped inside, and Runningdeer pushed the button for the eighth floor. "Bill, don't do anything I wouldn't do," Luther Steel cautioned.

"If they didn't want us going up, they sure won't want us getting off. These won't be the regular guys," Clark

Pietrowski advised. "Lay even money O'Brien's SWAT team is upstairs waiting for us."

"They can talk tough—" Luther Steel said.

"How about assaulting an officer?"

"Fine, Clark. Let them call a federal marshal to arrest me, then."

"Do they have to do that?" Runningdeer asked, the elevator slowing.

"I'm on official business," Steel told them, taking his badge from the inside of his breast pocket and clipping it to the outside.

The elevator stopped. The doors opened.

Clark Pietrowski laughed a little. "Too bad nobody took that bet."

No O'Brien, but four men in Metro SWAT gear stood just outside the elevator doors.

# CHAPTER
# 7

The wig felt hot and made her hair and scalp itch, but she realized the latter sensation was only psychosomatic, as was the feeling of butterflies in her stomach. She had never liked wigs, even when they were fashionable. She had owned one once, worn it a few times, then let it occupy drawer space. The cause of the butterflies was at once less complex and more real. She was unarmed on the streets of Metro for the first time in her adult life.

Even before it was legal to do so, her policeman father had decreed she should carry a gun in her purse. In those days it had been the little Model 60 Chiefs she carried these days in a shoulder holster. Once she'd joined the police department, she had upgraded her armament.

She half expected that someone would jump from behind one of the trash Dumpsters and try to rape her, the hospital being in the worst possible part of town, but if someone did, that someone would be in for a big, permanent shock.

She had begun martial-arts training as a young girl, continued it year after year and belt after belt, continued it even now in hiding as a member of the outlawed Patriots. She never deluded herself that if a three-hundred-pound man grabbed her, she could break him in two like a board. And he might get her, but not before she had gouged out his eyes, crushed his larynx, and all but neutered him.

The emergency entrance docks had a lot of cops hanging around them, and she recognized some of them. The forensic science people were here, too.

A murder?

Rosie Shepherd kept walking, the beautician's shoes she'd borrowed pinching her toes but less than the other white shoes had done. She wondered absently if big feet just went with being a cop, whether one were male or female.

She climbed the stairs, and a young man who looked as if he were just out of rookie status tried to stop her. "There's an emergency—see?" She showed him the electronic pager from the pocket of her dress. She didn't wait for an answer, simply slipped past him with a smile and walked through a rush of cold air into the emergency room reception area. She gave a knowing nod to the two women behind the counter and walked through the swinging doors, into the corridor beyond. It was green and gray and smelled of disinfectant.

She kept walking, hugging her hands to her arms below the short sleeves of the dress, the air conditioning making her suddenly freezing, the flesh of her arms goose-pimpling. Or maybe the knowledge that she was inside and still had to get back outside was doing it to her.

Rosie Shepherd, her toes cramped, kept walking. The surgical elevators were ahead. She would use those to get to the ICU on eight. . . .

* * *

"And so I'm under orders, sir, to ask you and these other two gentlemen to leave this floor at once."

Luther Steel had let the SWAT team man talk. And now it was his turn. "I'm here on official business, and I think federal matters take precedence here, sir."

"I only have my orders."

"Good for you," Luther Steel told him. "I'm not going to keep standing in the elevator to discuss this. We're stepping out." For the last minute the elevator had been shuddering, the doors trying to close, Clark Pietrowski working the door button to keep them open. Luther Steel stepped through, almost pushing his way past the mustached, flak-vested police officer. "Where's O'Brien?"

"SWAT's pretty busy these days, sir."

Metro SWAT had recently tripled its numbers as well, but Steel had serious doubts concerning its abilities since logic dictated the men could not have received adequate training in so short a time. "Whose orders are you under?"

The elevator doors closed with a pneumatic slap.

The Metro SWAT man's eyes hardened as he answered, "Direct orders of Deputy Commander Kaminsky, sir."

"How many are you?"

"Enough, sir."

"That wasn't an answer, Officer. That was a challenge." Each of the SWAT men wore a handgun, just a standard service revolver at that, and each had some type or another of fantasy fighting knife of cheap-looking quality. But there were no automatic weapons. "We are going through, with every intention of seeing Mrs. Harriet Evans and, if her physicians agree, talking with her. You know exactly why I'm here, and I know exactly why you're here. And since this is a matter of national security, I suggest you contact Ralph Kaminsky and tell him just what I said. I'll give you two minutes, and we're going through. Got it?"

"You're not passing, sir."

"You make your phone call; you've already blown about fifteen seconds, Officer."

Pietrowski's cigarette lighter made a loud clicking sound, and the mustached SWAT spokesman's left cheek twitched. The man's right hand moved to his gun. "Don't be—" Steel didn't have the chance to get out the word *stupid.* Steel's left hand shoved hard against the SWAT spokesman's chest, knocking him off-balance. The man's revolver came out of the leather duty holster.

Steel's right hand was moving faster: His coat was cleared; the Sig-Sauer P-226 was in his right fist and coming up on line. He heard Bill Runningdeer advise, "Nobody moves!" and there was the sound of the Uzi's bolt being slammed open for dramatic emphasis. The muzzle of Steel's pistol was an inch away from the tip of the mustached man's nose. The jaw slacked. Steel's left fist closed on the collar of the flak vest. Runningdeer spoke again. "Hand off that revolver, mister!"

Steel shoved the man away, looking for Pietrowski. Gun in hand, Pietrowski was running along the corridor. Steel broke into a sprint after him, calling back, "Bill! Disarm those men and use their handcuffs to restrain them; then follow after me!"

"Yes, sir!"

Pietrowski disappeared around the corner, holstering his revolver as he ran. A second later there was a burst of automatic-weapons fire, and Steel thought for a second that Kaminsky's men had been put under orders to shoot. "Kaminsky, you asshole!"

Pietrowski was crouched in a doorway, his revolver at raised pistol position, a chunk of wall three feet in front of him blown away by gunfire. Men in mixed BDUs and ski masks at the far end of the corridor stood by the swinging doors leading into the ICU. The door of one of the surgical elevators was opening. There were eight men at least, and one of them—a Uzi in his right fist— wheeled toward the elevator door. A pretty white woman, a nurse, was framed in the doorway for an instant, her hands in the pockets of her dress. As the muzzle of the Uzi came on line with her, Steel opened fire, two double taps. The man with the Uzi took all four hits. His body jerked with each shot fired. The woman spilled to the floor, rolling under his gun. She came up, wheeled right on her right foot, her left leg snapping up and outward, kicking the already falling man in the side of the head. The muzzle of the Uzi jerked upward, the gun still firing. She spun a full 360 degrees and kicked the Uzi out of his hands. As he fell, she dived for the gun.

Six of the ski-masked men ran off down the corridor while a seventh man in a ski mask, an M-16 in his hands, moved on her. Clark Pietrowski shouted, "Watch out for me, Luther!" then stepped out into the corridor as Steel swung his pistol on line. But Pietrowski's L-Frame .357 Magnum Smith was already firing, its report earsplittingly loud in the confines of the corridor. The man with the M-16 took the hit, and his body jackknifed, rear end crashing against a cart, overturning it. A third man was running toward the two men who were already down. Like the others, he was dressed in the informal but customary uniform of the FLNA. The woman stepped from a doorway she had dodged into and fired the Uzi point-blank into his chest and neck, and his body jerked back, his feet flying out from under him.

She picked up the third FLNAer's gun, threw down the nearly fired-out Uzi, and ran along the corridor in the direction from which the third man had come.

Steel was already running after her, shouting, "Clark, check these three!" As he looked back, he saw Bill Runningdeer coming after him, a few paces behind, jumping over one of the dead men, skinning out of his raincoat, the Uzi in his left fist.

The corridor took another bend. The woman disappeared around it. As Steel reached the bend, he saw her, crouched in a doorway, her dress bunched up to her thighs, the expropriated M-16's stock to her shoulder. Steel dodged into the opposite doorway as gunfire sprayed across the floor between them, an Uzi from the sound of it. Was there a way from here into the ICU? He didn't know.

Behind him, he heard Runningdeer shout, "Stay back!" and there was the sound of Runningdeer's Uzi cutting into an FLNAer who was stepping out to fire. The man went down, and the woman in the nurse's uniform broke into a run, to the end of the corridor. She tucked back, peered around the corner, then disappeared.

There was the sound of more gunfire where the woman had turned, and Steel went after her. Two FLNAers were boxed in beside swinging doors at the end of a short corridor. The rest of Kaminsky's SWAT people, three of them, faced the FLNA. Each side fired at the other. One of the FLNA men took a burst but still fired. The three SWAT men went down.

The woman was trapped behind a laundry cart that was half shot away. Luther Steel dropped into a roll, the Sig still in his right fist. The Smith revolver had been ripped from under his left armpit and was in his left fist as he came out of the roll. Both guns fired down the corridor as he acquired the targets, spraying. He shouted, "Back here, miss!" He could see the woman at the edge of his peripheral vision, but she wasn't running for cover. She was spraying the M-16 around the edge of the laundry cart.

Both FLNA men were down. Steel pocketed the revolver—no time to bother with it. The woman sprinted down the hall ahead of him, toward the swinging doors. As he dumped the spent fifteen-round magazine from the Sig, he heard Clark Pietrowski shout from behind him, "With that karate shit, that's gotta be Rosie Shepherd, Luther! Nail her gently!"

Steel skidded on his heels at the end of the corridor near the swinging doors, for a second feeling like a kid on an icy sidewalk. He hadn't tried it in years and almost lost his balance. He went through the doors in a roll, a twenty-round spare going up the Sig's magazine well, his thumb dropping the slide release.

There was the sound of a scream to his right from glass-partitioned offices. One of the partitions shattered as a woman in a nurse's uniform and a green surgical gown came through the glass, splaying out onto the tile floor. A man in a ski mask raised up, an M-16 coming on line. Steel fired; Pietrowski's .357 boomed from his left; Runningdeer's Uzi fired from his right. The body of the man in the ski mask flipped back over the partition top and through the glass, disappearing into the next cubicle.

Steel was up, Runningdeer and Pietrowski flanking him.

A burst of automatic-weapons fire. There was still one unaccounted-for FLNAer, at least one. And no time to check the man they'd just shot.

They framed themselves on both sides of another set of swinging doors. Pietrowski speed-loaded his revolver.

Runningdeer put a fresh magazine into the Uzi. Steel reloaded the 66, the little Smith back in his left fist. "Go for it, Clark!" Pietrowski grabbed a chair and hurtled it through. Runningdeer went in after it, crossing right to left. Steel crossed left to right just after him.

The woman Pietrowski had called Rosie Shepherd, a dishwater-blond wig and nurse's cap on the floor, was wrestling a man in a ski mask for an H&K MP-5 submachine gun.

Before Steel could react, the woman's right hand reached out, and she ducked. Steel started to fire at the ski-masked man's head. But the woman's right hand snapped up and outward, a hypodermic syringe in its fist, ramming it into the man's left eye.

There was a scream that didn't sound human. The submachine gun discharged through the window beside them, glass spraying outward, and fell from his hands, both hands ripping away the ski mask and the needle simultaneously.

"Holy shit!" Runningdeer shouted.

The man was Achmed Ferrazzi, one of the most wanted terrorists in the world. Steel threw himself toward Ferrazzi, who had a pistol. The woman wheeled away, then jumped. As Steel went to grab for Ferrazzi, the woman's right foot connected with Ferrazzi's jaw. The pistol discharged into the ceiling. Ferrazzi's head whiplashed back, and his body toppled through the window as Steel crashed into the wall, his right hand grabbing at Ferrazzi's BDU front. Steel's fingernails felt as if they were being ripped out. The fabric tore, two buttons popped across his field of vision as if in slow motion, and then Ferazzi's body was just gone.

Steel sagged toward the window, watching Ferrazzi fall.

An ambulance was parked eight floors below in the parking lot. Ferrazzi's body impacted on the roof of the vehicle and bounced; the roof seemed to collapse under him as he crashed downward again. The roof shattered inward, and Ferrazzi's body flopped to the parking lot surface beside it, bounced once, then was still.

Luther Steel breathed.

Behind him he heard Clark Pietrowski laugh, then say, "Hey, Rosie! So where ya been keepin' yourself?"

"Around, Clark. How're the wife and the grandchildren?"

"Kids are growin' like weeds, ya know!"

Luther Steel closed his eyes and shook his head.

The small talk continued. He opened his eyes, turned around, and looked at the woman. She was peeling something that looked like a cross between a large rubber band and a hairnet off her head, and her own hair, a kind of auburn color that was pretty common among white women but looked attractive nonetheless, fell to her shoulders. She shook her head several times, the hair tossing.

"I'm Special Agent Luther Steel, Detective Shepherd—" But as he started to speak, Luther Steel looked at the woman on the bed.

Runningdeer was bending over her.

"Three or four rounds in the pump," Pietrowski said. "Judging from the make of subgun, three. Somebody wanted Mrs. Evans pretty bad."

"Why?" Steel asked, looking at Rose Shepherd.

"You know why, or at least you can guess, can't you?"

She was a pretty woman, and he guessed tougher than most men. "What were you doing here?"

"Came to visit a sick friend."

"I believe that you did," Steel told her. "And Mrs. Evans was the friend. Why?"

"Boss, we're gonna have a lot of company in a couple of minutes. Those guys on the first floor are—"

"What's going on?" Detective Shepherd asked, her eyes narrowing.

Steel looked at his watch. "Stall, Clark. Bill, get that submachine gun out of sight until after the police arrive. Detective Shepherd? How about an elevator ride?"

"The surgery elevators are the only chance. But why am I telling you that?"

"Show me," Luther Steel told her, taking her elbow and starting to propel her out of the room.

# CHAPTER
# 8

There was something wrong, because Rosie wasn't wearing the wig and there were sirens in the distance and a tall, good-looking black man was walking beside her. And she was carrying a dark-finished automatic pistol in one hand and a shiny little revolver in the other, but both hands were at her sides.

David Holden reached for one of his own handguns. He stepped out of the van, the full-size Beretta in his right fist. "Rosie?"

"David! Listen to him!"

"I'm Special Agent Luther Steel, Professor Holden. Hear me out, then kill me if you feel you must. She's got both my guns, and they're loaded! But listen to me first!"

"Rosie!"

"David, I think he's on our side! David, please!"

"Those are Metro police and probably some military you hear coming. There are eight dead FLNAers in the ICU and three dead Metro cops. By the time this is over, I may be in as much trouble as you are. But Rudolph Cerillia wants me to talk with you. Please, sir!"

David Holden trusted Rosie Shepherd more than any-one living. "Rudolph Cerillia?"

"Can we talk inside your van, Professor?"

Rosie's shoulders were raised, her arms limp at her sides, a look of helpless frustration on her face.

"Rosie?"

"Listen to him."

"And that van had better be moving. My two men back up on the eighth floor will steer the police in the wrong direction and give them the wrong description. But we can't count on that for long. In ten minutes or less this entire area will be sealed so tightly, a flea couldn't get out."

The black man, his hands palms open and away from his sides, stopped walking.

"Let's go for a ride," David Holden said, then stepped back up into the van.

# CHAPTER

# 9

They parked the van off the road in a wooded area of mixed evergreen and deciduous trees twenty-five miles northeast of Metro and five miles from the interstate, then began to walk, Holden holding Rosie Shepherd's hand. She hadn't changed clothes, still wore the nurse's uniform, but had changed into her combat boots, the combination of dress, white stockings, and black eight-inch boots looking charmingly stupid, Holden thought.

Holden had left his coat in the van. The sun was warm and his shirtsleeves were rolled up, his armpits damp under the shoulder holster's harness. Steel had removed his coat as well. Steel's shoulder holster was ringed with perspiration. But the black FBI agent's holsters were empty.

"The director wants to meet with you personally, both of you."

"He met us," Holden said noncommittally.

"You're the ones who saved his life. He told us that after he came out of surgery. But he'd wanted to meet with you before any of that happened. He'd assigned me to head up a task force that would find you, arrange such a meeting."

Flies buzzed; leaves from last autumn and dried twigs snapped under their feet as they walked. Last autumn, Holden remembered, his wife and children had been alive; none of this had happened.

Rosie Shepherd asked Steel, "Are you saying Cerillia is willing to turn this thing around?"

"As I outlined to you back in the ICU after Mr. Ferrazzi left us so abruptly, Detective Shepherd, Mr. Cerillia will cover the specifics. But yes, he believes in the Patriots as a source for help in these troubled times, as does the President. He doesn't consider the Patriots public enemies. But official policy is official policy. He'll have to talk with you both to explain it."

Rosie said suddenly, "He wants to talk to David. Talking to me is just to make David comfortable, right?"

Steel looked away, squinting in the sunlight. "It's beautiful out here. I almost envy you people, not being chained to a desk most of the time like me."

"Answer her," Holden hissed.

"All right. Yes. It was assumed from the outset that Rufus Burroughs is dead. Am I correct?"

Holden said nothing.

Steel went on. "And if Sergeant Burroughs was dead, then it was assumed that one of the two of you would take over leadership of the Patriot cell here in Metro. There have been many famous women guerrilla leaders, but more often, if a man and a woman are equally in line for the leadership role, the woman has deferred to the man, perhaps exercising as much of a leadership function as the man, but through him. If you want Detective Shepherd—"

"No—" Her hand went rigid in his, but she kept walking.

"Shut up, Rosie. She comes if I come. But neither one

of us comes to any meeting unless we're sure it isn't a
trap. This thing with Cerillia sounds too good to be true,
and when something sounds too good to be true, that
usually means that it is."

"Why did I walk Detective Shepherd out of that hospital using my badge as a cover and then give her my guns?
Ever hear the word *trust*?" And Luther Steel stopped
walking.

David Holden had known the word once.

# CHAPTER
## 10

Rudolph Cerillia's stomach was totally empty; it had to be because he had vomited so often there could be nothing left in it. As he stepped down from the last tread of the foldout steps built into the business-size jet aircraft's passenger door, he thought of the frequently seen newsreel image of the pope, dropping to his knees and touching his lips reverently to the ground. Cerillia was almost tempted to do the same, but not out of deference or in a gesture of blessing to Metro, where his plane had landed in a small airport just outside the city. He felt like kissing the ground because he was at last returned to it. Airplanes—even the thought of riding in one—made him physically ill. He had tried becoming as knowledgeable as he could concerning airplanes, he had tried hypnosis, he had tried everything one could try, and after all that, he always traveled by train unless some matter demanded such immediate attention that flying was the only option left him.

The telephone call from Luther Steel was such a matter.

Cerillia stood at the base of the steps, holding on to the

hand railing, his left arm still aching when he exerted too much pressure with it. He was trying to get his legs fully under him again while the black Lincoln Towncar idled twenty yards or so away and his new administrative assistant, Tim Kjelstrom, started tending to the overnight bags each of them had hastily packed.

It had taken vastly longer than Cerillia had hoped for Luther Steel to make solid contact with David Holden, but vastly less time than logic had dictated Cerillia had any right to expect that it should.

"Mr. Cerillia, I've got—"

Cerillia waved Kjelstrom away for a moment, controlling his breathing, trying to determine if his stomach had settled enough yet that he could walk to the car. To risk talking was out of the question. He looked at the aircraft, regarding it on a purely emotional basis, like some sort of malevolent entity. If he took the drugs his doctor had prescribed for motion sickness, to calm his nerves of the fear which consumed him, he was worthless for several hours afterward. Hence he never took the drugs.

Cerillia rationalized that it was not so damning that he had one terrible mental quirk; so many others had so many more, some of which were damning indeed. His was merely an inconvenience and an embarrassment.

He shook his head, belched, covered his mouth with his hand, then pushed himself unsteadily away from the handrail and started toward the car.

"Come on, Kjelstrom," he said, finally managing a few words, his throat feeling raw from all that had gone past it in the last few hours. He had been in Santa Fe, New Mexico, when the call had tracked him down. The moment he had decided he would travel to Metro via aircraft, the sick feelings in his stomach had started. He had vomited once even before leaving his hotel. A young agent Cerillia vaguely recognized held the Lincoln's door open for him, and he nodded and grunted a "thank you" and sank down into the seat.

Once more he'd made it down alive. . . .

It was one of those motels where all the rooms are on the first floor because at least at the time that it was built, there had been an abundance of real estate to waste and it was cheaper to expand outward than upward.

Cerillia got out of the car. The motel parking lot was dimly lit, but it was easy enough to see; he'd refined his night vision in the back alleys of Chicago as a cop. He glanced back once at the Lincoln. Tim Kjelstrom and the local agent, a man named William Runningdeer, were waiting beside the car. He'd remembered Runningdeer, about ten minutes into the drive between the rural airfield and here, as one of the men Steel had handpicked for his task force. Outside the motel room door Cerillia saw one of the other men, lounging in the shadows, a lit cigarette in his fingers. He was Clark Pietrowski, the only Metro area agent Luther Steel had trusted to include in his special unit.

Pietrowski threw away his cigarette and stood up straighter, saying, "Mr. Cerillia. A real honor, sir."

"Pietrowski. Hear you guys were in quite a gunfight."

"As gunfights go, it was okay, sir. Those Metro cops were a bunch of jerks."

"Inside there?" And Rudolph Cerillia gestured dismissively toward the motel room door nearest Pietrowski.

"Yes, sir." Pietrowski walked over to the door and knocked some sort of secret knock, three raps and then two and then three more.

Cerillia experienced mild surprise when a woman opened the door. She was dressed in a white short-sleeved blouse open at the throat and a light blue skirt that came down to her ankles. There was a black pistol in her right hand that he guessed was a .45 automatic, and apparently recognizing his face, she made the pistol disappear behind the fullness of her skirt.

"Come in, Mr. Cerillia."

"You must be Detective Shepherd."

"I used to be. You're ruining the air conditioning."

Cerillia nodded and stepped inside. Rose Shepherd's auburn hair was caught up in a ponytail at the crown of her head, with one of those rubber-band things with balls on each end wound around it, he noticed, as she glanced away from him for a second. Cerillia followed her eyes.

Luther Steel was standing up. Sitting beside him near the drawn window curtains but in the shadow beyond the cone of overhead light was another man. Cerillia recognized the face: lean, high cheekbones; dark wavy hair; dark penetrating eyes. It was the face he had last seen aboard the train bound from Metro to New Orleans, the face of the man who had saved his life by risking his own to kill the assassin sent by the FLNA to eliminate a troublesome FBI director.

"Professor Holden."

"Mr. Director."

"You're looking better than you did the last time. A head wound, I seem to recall."

"A lot of blood, but head wounds always do that. A mild concussion. But I'm fully restored. You're looking quite a bit better, too."

"My left arm's about half as good as it used to be, but my doctors and the physical therapy people say that in time I, too, will be restored."

The woman cleared her throat.

Luther Steel crossed the few steps to him. "May I get you a chair, Mr. Director?"

"I'd rather stand, Luther. Thanks."

David Holden stood up, and Cerillia could see the leader of the Patriot cell in Metro more clearly. He wore a button-down white shirt, the sleeves rolled up past the elbows, a black knit tie at half mast below the open collar, a shoulder holster harness over his shoulders, a pistol under the left arm, what looked like spare magazines and an inverted knife under the right arm. A second pistol was thrust almost casually into the waistband of his trousers in front of the left hipbone. The second pistol, at least, was one of the large-capacity Berettas.

Cerillia extended his right hand. David Holden made the same gesture. Holden's handshake was strong, but not overly so. "You have no idea how long I've wanted this meeting to take place," Cerillia said.

The knocking came at the door again. It was the same pattern as before when Clark Pietrowski had announced his arrival. Cerillia turned toward the door. Rose Shepherd was already cracking the curtain a bit to peer outside. Her pistol, cocked and locked, was stuffed into the waistband of her skirt at the small of her back. The position was dangerous, Cerillia had always felt, but fast. And perhaps "dangerous" was an apt description for Rose Shepherd.

The door opened. Clark Pietrowski stepped into the doorway, handing Rose Shepherd two off-white flat boxes approximately twenty inches square. The door closed, and Rose Shepherd turned to face into the room. "We got two for your people outside."

"Delivery pizza's a luxury for us these days," David Holden announced.

Rudolph Cerillia couldn't help himself, and he just

started to laugh. And he looked at Luther Steel. "Is the government treating?" he asked.

Steel looked down at his shoes and grinned. . . .

Dimitri Borsoi caught sight of his own reflection in the mirror. What he saw did not make him happy.

Achmed Ferrazzi and some of the best fighters from the Leopards were dead. But at least so was Harriet Evans.

"Who told the FBI about her?"

Borsoi looked away from his own image and toward the disagreeably bland visage of Humphrey Hodges. "Someone at the hospital or more likely someone in local law enforcement. That one policeman is dead, at any event. But stopping a leak after the damage is nearly done is hardly effective. We have to win the election, and the only way to do that is by disrupting the process so severely that our candidate cannot help winning."

"But what if the people become so outraged by the violence that they elect Roger Costigan, Mr. Johnson? What happens then?"

Dimitri Borsoi sat down opposite Hodges's desk and looked out the window behind the desk and into the night. What would happen then indeed?

"This conversation can never leave this room. To put my case very frankly, sir, the President has ordered me to strike this arrangement with you. And I am in cheerful compliance," Rudolph Cerillia said, putting down a half-eaten slice of pizza. "His sentiments wholeheartedly echo my own. This is not a conventional problem presented to us by the Front for the Liberation of North America. Whatever the inspiration, we have the effect of a full-blown revolution on our hands. Therefore, because the problem is not conventional, conventional solutions don't seem to be the answer. Police and military and even much of federal law enforcement seem to be ineffective." Luther Steel's eyes looked as though they had just taken a slap. "For every effective operation we have, such as Special Agent Steel's activities, we have a dozen that aren't." Steel's expression softened. He was very good-looking, and his face read like a book for the visually impaired. It was all in his dark brown eyes, really. "The inevitable conclusion seems that we take advantage of an operation that is proving effective, trying to aid its efficient disposition of the crisis at hand rather than road-blocking it. We want, in short, to work with you and Detective Shepherd and the rest of the Patriot organization. And that has to start with the two of you and your cell. The Patriots need effective overall leadership. You can provide that, and behind the scenes, never openly, we can provide all the assistance possible to aid your efforts at combating the FLNA."

David Holden wiped his hands on a napkin. Rose Shepherd wanted to tell him, "Right there, by the corner of your mouth," because there was a tiny splotch of tomato sauce there. He was the best-looking man she had ever seen, even when he was wounded and dirty and tired and all he wanted to do was sleep in her arms. He wiped his mouth with the napkin, and the blemishing tomato sauce was no longer of concern.

"You didn't eat very much, Mr. Cerillia," David remarked.

"I'm lucky to be able to eat at all. As you're probably aware, I don't normally ride trains out of a fascination with nostalgia."

"I think Mr. Cerillia's flight here tonight shows the importance with which he views this meeting, Professor

Holden. And the esteem in which he holds you and Detective Shepherd," Steel added, swallowing pizza.

Talk turned to the most recent atrocities of the FLNA: the church bombings in the Pacific Northwest; the airliner sabotage which had caused the deaths of 497 people, 20 of them teenagers and members of a gymnastics team traveling aboard a commercial jet that was blown out of the sky. There were the assassinations of several political figures in the Midwest, mainly candidates for public office in municipal elections.

Rosie's hands were folded in her lap, palms upward; her knees were tight together. She looked down at the floor; her feet vanished beneath the hem of her skirt. She looked up. She watched Rudolph Cerillia, wondering if she should trust this man. Cerillia said, "With the elections coming in Metro in just a short while, things should get much hotter down here. This will be a good means for us to work out any bugs in the system I propose and to throw a monkey wrench into FLNA plans to disrupt the election."

David Holden remained silent, and she watched his eyes. Was he asking himself the same questions she was about the FBI director and his presidential orders?

"Harris Ganby isn't exactly the ideal candidate, but there doesn't seem to be any connection between him and the FLNA, at least not that any intelligence data we have would suggest," Cerillia went on. "And Roger Costigan seems the perfect choice for these perilous times."

For some reason Rose Shepherd looked at David. He smiled, not at her but at something he was thinking. "When I was in college, people used to joke about 'perilous times' speeches. And those were perilous times. But nothing compared with now. And who knows what lies ahead? Roger Costigan is a right-wing demagogue, as opposed to Harris Ganby, who seems like a nebbish. So we have Mr. Law and Order or we have Mr. Wishy-washy. Increasingly often the trouble with elections these days is that no one runs that people in their right minds would want to elect. The one consolation is that whoever wins at least isn't out there on the street anymore. Sometimes I think government buildings need locks on the outside, rather like patient rooms in mental institutions." Rose Shepherd wanted to get up and give him a kiss, but she sat right where she was.

Cerillia said nothing for a moment, then commented: "It's the American way."

"Electing imbeciles? Hardly. Self-serving politicians don't govern; they mismanage, self-perpetuate, and endure. There are a great number of men and women in elected positions who embody the best spirit of this nation. But they are frustrated at every turn by the ones who are in it for cushy jobs. And more and more, men and women who could serve this country well refuse to become involved in the sordid mess the others keep expanding. Maybe someday, if any good ever comes of these times, the people who could do something, who place the American people and this nation above personal greed and the desire for power, will get disgusted enough that they will run for office in greater numbers. Return government to what it should be. Little choice between a Costigan and a Ganby, a blowhard and a wimp, isn't there?"

Cerillia was silent for a long few seconds. Rose Shepherd was suddenly aware of the sounds of her own breathing. Then, his voice lower than she had ever heard it, Cerillia said, "You don't mince words, do you, Professor Holden?"

"Why should I? Why should anyone?"

"So what if you're right? Is it still worth fighting for? The United States?"

"If you thought you needed to ask me that question, Mr. Director, I doubt you'd be here."

She looked at David Holden. It was his soul that touched her as much as his body.

# CHAPTER

# 11

Personal charge of the situation was the thing. Whoever became the new mayor of Metro, it seemed obvious that a first step would be dismissal of the commander. And to bring in an outside man from another city would be not only demoralizing to the citizenry and the police but also patently impractical. He was the logical man to become commander, had served with distinction as deputy commander, had put up with all the problems, had made the decisions. He was the logical man.

"Mr. Kaminsky?"

"What? Oh—"

The right passenger door was wide open, and O'Brien, looking at him oddly, was leaning inside. "There are other matters besides this raid to attend to when you're deputy commander for Metro PD, O'Brien."

"Yes, sir. We're ready now. But if you don't mind my saying so, sir, there's no reason you should risk your own safety—"

Did O'Brien want the job? After all, commander of Metro SWAT was a high-profile position, face always in the papers and all over the evening newscasts these days. Had it been wise to triple the size of O'Brien's command?

"Sir, I really think—"

"It's your job to carry out plans like this. I appreciate your concern, but we can't afford to have anything go wrong. And that's the end of it."

"Yes, sir. Then you'd better get ready."

He knew that. He wasn't a fool. He picked up the SWAT vest from the seat beside him and stepped out of the Cadillac into the warm summer night. Ralph Kaminsky suddenly realized he wasn't quite sure how to put on the vest. Was this thing made for a woman or something? It looked as if it buttoned over on the wrong side, from right to left. He turned it around in his hands.

"Could I help you, sir?"

Kaminsky sniffed and looked O'Brien in the eye. The craggy face, the almost-out-of-regs mustache, the black Battle Dress Utilities, the black baseball cap with the METRO SWAT brassard, all the gear on his vest. Kaminsky thought he had it. He started into it. But he still couldn't figure out how it closed.

"You close the snaps, sir, then fold the Velcro over," O'Brien said in a low voice.

"It doesn't take a genius to figure that out," Kaminsky snapped. He had the thing closed. It felt heavier on than it had in his hands. "These are my rifle clips?" He patted the pouches on either side of the abdomen portion.

"Spare magazines for your submachine gun, sir. And these pouches are for spare pistol magazines. We fitted you with a Beretta."

He knew about Berettas. He'd read the James Bond novels years ago, and he read the police magazines.

O'Brien reached under his vest and produced another handgun, did something with it that made clicking noises, then handed it over. The top of the pistol was locked back, and when Kaminsky took it in hand, he could look down inside and see cartridges. He realized he had no idea what to do with it. When he'd been a uniform policeman—and that hadn't lasted long—everyone carried the same gun. It was a good policy, but now—

"Sir, that lever on the left. Push that down with your thumb and—"

Kaminsky pushed down the lever and felt pain across the fleshy part of the back of his hand, between the thumb and first finger. "Damn thing!"

"Here, sir." O'Brien worked some kind of lever on the pistol and said, "There, sir. It goes into the holster there on the right side of the vest."

"Yes."

"We'll be waiting, sir." O'Brien walked off.

Kaminsky shifted the gun into his left hand. His right hand still stung from the gun closing. It was all right for O'Brien. O'Brien wore gloves.

Kaminsky felt around on his right side. There was a holster there. There was a safety strap. He got the gun into the holster; but the safety strap had some kind of funny plastic buckle on it, and it wouldn't close properly. "Damn."

There was nothing for it. Officers always lead their men into battle with just a pistol in hand. He retook the pistol in his right hand. There was a baseball cap just like O'Brien's on the seat, and Kaminsky leaned back inside, took it, put it on his head, catching his reflection in the window. He adjusted the angle. It looked better cocked slightly downward over one eye.

Ralph Kaminsky knew the game. After the shooting was over, and there probably wouldn't be much of that, the reporters would be called. And then he'd announce that the Patriots who were responsible for the death of Evans, the newsman, had been apprehended or killed.

Gun in hand, he strode toward the black vans and destiny.

# CHAPTER

## 12

The lights from the motels and closed-for-the-night fast-food restaurants at the interchange vanished in an instant as the Ford he drove crossed over the brow of the hill and down into the gradually sloping valley.

His right hand squeezed both of Rosie Shepherd's hands, resting in her lap as she sat pressed beside him. His left hand was bunched at the top of the steering wheel. They turned off the U.S. highway onto the state-maintained two-lane blacktop, his headlights sweeping back on line with a jerk as he recovered the wheel. Rosie's head rested against his right arm and shoulder, and David Holden wasn't quite certain if she was still awake. A loose wisp of hair touched his cheek.

He felt like a kid, tooling along a deserted highway well into the predawn hours, one hand on the steering wheel, one hand on the girl, the girl he loved.

At first he'd thought it was merely a reaction to the loneliness that the loss of wife and children all in the span of a few minutes had wreaked on him. But as the weeks had worn by, he realized that what he felt for Rosie Shepherd was a love as genuine as the love he had felt for

Elizabeth, his wife. Sometimes that frightened him because if something were to happen to Rosie Shepherd, inside himself Holden knew he would be alone for the rest of his life. She was his second chance, and there wouldn't be a third.

Partly because of Rosie beside him and partly, too, because of the satisfactory conclusion of an agreement of sorts with Federal Bureau of Investigation Director Rudolph Cerillia and, through Cerillia, the President, for the first time since the death of his family David Holden saw hope. It was still a hazy image, but hope was there.

"Whatcha thinking?" Rosie's voice sounded small, a little afraid perhaps.

"About you mostly."

"I was asleep."

"I kind of noticed," Holden half whispered, holding her hands more tightly.

Holden felt Rosie's lips touch softly at his right cheek near the corner of his mouth. "I was proud of you tonight. You stood up for what you believe in, what I believe in, too." She cleared her throat.

Holden let go of her hands, raised his arm, and enfolded her in it. Her head came down against his chest. "When I was a street cop," she said, "if I saw people driving like this, I knew I should probably pull them over. I should warn them you needed both hands on the wheel. But I never could make myself do it," she concluded in an almost conspiratorial whisper, a slight catch in her throat.

His right hand rested over her right breast, and she scrunched closer to him, pulling the white sweater that was over her shoulders over his hand and closer around her. "It got cool. Maybe the heat will break."

"Yeah. Maybe," Holden whispered. "I love you, but I bet you figured that out."

"Uh-huh." She laughed.

They were nearing the turnoff, and Holden said to her, "Why don't you hold my arm? I need both hands for this crazy road."

He took his arm from around her, and her hands folded across his right bicep. "This could be the chance. With the President and the FBI and everybody behind us, maybe we can end this thing," Rosie Shepherd said very softly.

"But it's all unofficial," Holden reminded her grimly. "If this President goes out of office before it's over, we could wind up with a totally different situation and probably a totally different man in charge of the FBI."

"I love you."

"I know," Holden told her, leaning over her quickly, kissing her hair.

"Hmm." She sighed.

David Holden started to say something, but then he realized that the sounds he'd heard so softly for the last thirty seconds or so, that he'd almost been unaware of hearing at all, were the sounds of gunfire. He cut the wheel right and drew the Ford onto the shoulder, a hundred yards or so out from the turnoff onto the farm road along which their rendezvous lay. There was a raid scheduled this morning against a horse farm used by the FLNA as a guerrilla training camp.

A spray of gravel and dirt pelted the undercarriage, and the car skidded a little as he stopped nearly too quickly. He had already mechanically shut off the lights. And now he shut off the engine. Rosie Shepherd huddled close to him, and he looked down into her eyes. The moonlight was still bright enough to see the details of her face; the starlight, once distanced from the corona of the moon, was brilliant as well. He rolled down the window, listening to the night sounds: crickets; the buzzing of insects. He stared up into the sky.

And the gunfire came again.

"You stay with the car. Drive down the road. Maybe back to that all-night truck stop by the interstate and—"

"No. That's coming from—"

"I can't lose you. I know you're just as good at this stuff as I am, maybe a whole lot better, but I can't lose you. You understand that?" And Holden realized his hands were on her shoulders and he was squeezing her tightly and the sweater she wore had fallen away.

He had turned his body toward her, and her mouth was now inches from his. Holden drew her against him. "Do you understand that, Rosie?" And Holden bent his face over hers and touched his mouth to hers. Her breath was hot, her body warm under his hands; her breasts pressed hard against his chest. "If we get out of this—"

And her hands were on his face, and her mouth touched his mouth, his face, his hands, as his mouth touched her hair. Holden held her.

"Go on!" she told him, her voice sounding tight. "I'll wait there. Go on!"

He had the car door open. Rosie slid behind the wheel. She pulled the door closed, and as the car began accelerating, Holden stepped back, turning away to protect his face from the spray of loose gravel. Holden stood there for a second or so, watching after her.

He heard the sounds of gunfire again.

Holden looked down at his gray summer-weight slacks and city shoes. Despite it all, he felt a smile cross his lips, and he laughed at himself. The college history professor indeed.

He started down the embankment past the shoulder, then along the depression at its base until he found a natural ravine. He clambered along it diagonally and up toward the top of the embankment, then out into the tall grass beyond where it was never cut. Crickets made loudly protesting noises, and he heard the movement of something appreciably larger, perhaps a rabbit. Then he was into the trees.

Already the gunfire sounded louder and less sporadic here, its origin apparently slightly to the north of the clearing selected a week earlier for the staging area, closer, in fact, to the horse farm. He wondered. David Holden turned the collar of his sport coat up against the low-hanging tree limbs. His right hand drew the military Beretta from the small of his back; his left hand shagged away the larger branches as they swatted against him.

His shirt was already soaked with sweat, and the fronts of his thighs were a darker gray. The humidity was heavy on the air, and the cool breezes he'd felt on the highway had all but vanished here.

He kept moving, toward the gunfire.

Possible scenarios for the gunfire ran through his brain, but he always came back to the same one: that somehow his people had stumbled on to theirs, or theirs had stumbled on to his, and the kind of firefight that was the most brutal because it was the least expected had occurred.

David Holden quickened his pace as much as he dared.

# CHAPTER

# 13

The people who sold high-intensity lighting systems were the ones who had profited the most since the FLNA violence had begun. The truck stop's parking lot was a textbook example.

Rose Shepherd shut off the Ford's lights, then turned off the key switch.

She felt her shoulders sag and suddenly realized she was very cold. She took the white sweater from the seat beside her and, putting it around her shoulders, just sat there and stared across the lot toward the lighted restaurant. It was so bright inside that even considering the distance, she could almost make out some of the signs on the wall indicating what was on special.

Another industry which had thrived since the FLNA terror had begun was private security. A pair of rent-a-cop harness bulls was starting toward the car now. One of them held a white Styrofoam cup in his right hand and a cigarette in his left. Rose Shepherd wondered almost absently which hand was left for him to get to his gun with. The other one, the fatter of the two, though neither was exactly in fighting trim, had both thumbs hooked in his belt.

There was nothing to do but to get out of the car and go inside. A woman alone sitting in the parking lot at this time of the morning would only provoke problems. She looked at her watch. It was almost five thirty. She took the keys from the ignition and, rather than drop them into her purse, put them into the right-side slash pocket of her skirt. She might need them quickly.

She got out from behind the wheel, her purse going over her left shoulder. The sweater went across her shoulders again, and she snuggled it close around her. She was still a little cold with the breeze coming across the parking lot and playing with her skirt. She locked the Ford, turned away from the car, and started toward the restaurant, the two security guards on a direct intercept path with her.

To walk out of her way to avoid them would have made it worse. The breeze was blowing dead on toward her, molding her clothes against her legs. She noticed a smirk on the face of the one with the Stryofoam cup and the cigarette.

The distance between them was less than a dozen yards now. Mr. Preparedness called to her, "Kinda early, ain't it, girlie? Or is it jus' kinda late?" The fatter man laughed as though at some secret joke, but she caught the broad reference.

She kept walking. "A pretty baby like you—" Mr. Preparedness began.

There was always the chance they recognized her face from a wanted poster or from a newspaper or television, but temper got the better of her. She turned around abruptly. "Listen, asshole! My boyfriend chews up creeps tougher than you for breakfast, then spits them out. So back off or I'll turn him loose on both of you when he gets here." Neither man apparently knew what to say or looked immediately enthused about the prospects of meeting her "boyfriend," but she didn't want them getting a longer look at her than she had to, so she turned back toward the restaurant. She walked away, hugging the sweater more tightly around her. A smile crossed her lips. David was her boyfriend.

She pushed the heavy door open. Both hands and a shoulder were needed, and she didn't consider herself weak as women went. There was a little counter with a cash register and a glass-front display, the glass sparklingly clean. Inside the case she noticed everything from breath mints to prophylactics, both items in a wide range of styles.

The restaurant itself seemed nearly empty except for a few burly men in work clothes or cowboy shirts, easily matched with one or another of the vehicles she had seen parked in the lot. There was an empty booth in the middle of the row and about halfway along the length of the counter. Beside the windows it held a commanding view of the parking lot and of the Ford she'd driven here. To sit farther back and isolate herself from the few patrons made some sense, but less sense than sitting in prominent view, just in case the two rent-a-cops summoned up some nerve and started trouble. She could always pull the helpless woman routine and force the situation so one of the truck drivers would punch them out.

She swept her skirt under her as she sat down and looked at the menu. Over the top of the menu she saw the two security guards staring toward her. A lot of good people worked as rent-a-cops, but then there were guys like these. She tried to ignore them.

A waitress came over, a ruffled apron on over a clean

pink uniform, a ruffled handkerchief in a pocket over her left breast so small as to be useless. "What'll ya have, honey?"

Coffee might not last long enough. "Give me two eggs sunny-side up and toast. Potatoes instead of grits, okay?"

"Want coffee?"

"Yes, thank you."

"Right back with your coffee, honey."

Rose Shepherd put the menu into the little chrome-plated slots between the salt and pepper shakers and next to the sugar. She couldn't see Mr. Preparedness and his fat friend anymore, but just in case, she opened the button of her blouse just above the waistband of her skirt. The sweater was still draped across her shoulders. It covered her hand, which trailed inside across her abdomen and to the butt of the little Model 60 in the Ken Null holster beside her left breast. The revolver was easily in reach, and she withdrew her hand.

Her coffee arrived, and she smiled at the waitress. The waitress set down two little plastic containers of synthetic cream. Rose Shepherd sipped at her black coffee.

The door leading in from the parking lot opened. Two men came in. One of them was little more than a boy. She recognized him. He was one of the lower-echelon Leopards, just a punk with an acne problem and a foul mouth. She'd busted him once for possession and once for carrying an illegal knife; he'd tried stabbing her with it. She looked away, but not before the image of the second man registered with her. He was nice enough looking, tall. There was something indefinably foreign about him. He'd been making the rounds of the street gangs before the FLNA things had got started.

She was trying to remember the name she'd picked up

on him. At last she did, although it sounded like an alias. The name was Johnson.

Rose Shepherd sipped from the coffee cup held in her left hand as the two sat down at the counter fewer than ten feet from her. Her right hand was beside the opened button of her blouse.

# CHAPTER
## 14

The gunfire was originating from a deep ravine through which a shallow stream churned, the white water faintly luminescent in the grayish blackness. Men were hidden in the trees above the water, firing down toward the randomly strewn boulders about a hundred yards farther along the stream, from behind which other men fired. Bullets whined as they struck the rocks. Commands, so muted they were unintelligible, filtered from the trees and over the water. There were men on the near side of the ravine as well, and these men Holden recognized. They were his own, members of the Metro Patriot cell. They were firing toward the opposite side of the ravine; logic dictated that this was the enemy position.

The scenario was much as he had anticipated it would be. His force and an FLNA force from the nearby horse farm had somehow inadvertently encountered each other. The course of the ravine was one of the two infiltration routes selected for reaching the staging area. More of the Patriots had come to the sounds of the gunfire, and more of the FLNA had come as well. A quick and bloody skirmish was turning into a full-blown battle.

It could become worse. The FLNA could summon more help. But his people constituted the only Patriot cell operating in the Metro area. No help was available.

Holden started moving, the military Beretta going into the waistband of his torn and mud-stained city trousers, his right hand reaching up under his right arm, freeing the Crain Defender knife from its inverted sheath.

His fist balled over the haft. The handle was black, synthetic, seamless, and beneath this material, rope was bound over the block of stainless steel that was machined into a hollow tube used for holding survival necessities. The system Jack Crain used in its hand fabrication made the hollow-handled knife for all intents and purposes as strong as a full-tang knife.

Holden moved along the ridge until he reached the stream, well above the battle scene. The ground forming the embankment was clay mixed with gravel and some larger rocks. He started down, skidding because there was nothing for any footing. He half soaked himself in the stream bed, wading across, the footing here worse because of the slickness of the rocks. But he made it across without incident, and the far side of the ravine rose before him. He assayed it for a moment, shook his head, and started climbing. Almost halfway up, his footing went, and he reached out. The rock to which he held for an instant was dislodged. He stabbed the Defender down into the embankment; the nearly eight inches of steel which formed the blade bit deep but held. David Holden pulled himself upward, found a purchase for his feet, then wrenched the Defender free. He stabbed it down again as far above him as he could reach and pulled himself up with it. His left hand found a seemingly sturdy root, and he gouged his fingers into it for purchase, wrenched the Defender free, then heaved himself up and out of the ravine.

He got up to his knees, then to his feet. He grabbed a handful of maple leaves from a low-hanging branch as he ran past. He wiped the sand and clay from his knife with the maple leaves, then discarded them.

He was circling the enemy position in the trees overlooking the ravine. Because he was armed only with his pistols, to precipitate a counterattack from the rear would have been suicidal and pointless. He needed an assault rifle at the very least.

He would use the Crain Defender to get it.

Holden slowed his pace, well into the trees again, moving laterally, paralleling the ravine, along a line a hundred yards or better from the rearmost enemy position he had been able to detect.

There was a fresh deadfall tree spanning a natural hedge of long-thorned wild roses. Holden crept up onto the deadfall and moved slowly along it lest it dislodge and spill him to the ground. It saved ripping his flesh.

At the far end of the deadfall Holden crouched, the Defender tight in his fist.

A man shape to his left, the stutter of an M-16 on full auto with poor trigger control. Holden jumped down from the deadfall and remained perfectly still for a long moment.

He could see the man more clearly now, reloading with a fresh magazine.

As the man began again to fire, Holden started toward his back. He kept to a low crouch, friendly fire here ripping into the tree cover only a dozen or so yards ahead, but the angle wrong unless a ricochet caught him.

The distance to the man he intended to kill narrowed now to fewer than twenty-five yards. The gunfire from the ravine seemed somehow more intense, and Holden dropped to his knees and elbows, creeping along over the rotted leaf material and the bright green stringlike vines.

His left trouser leg—what there was left of it—caught in a thorn, and Holden shook it free, tearing skin and swearing under his breath. He kept moving, edging left into the taller wild oats, the man still shooting sporadically just ahead of him.

The palm of Holden's right hand was sweating, the Venus mound between the knuckles of his first finger and thumb bunched over the slightly oval-shaped guard.

Ten yards.

*The gunfire be damned,* he thought. If he crawled the remaining distance, he'd betray himself. Holden drew his knees up under him, rose into a crouch, looked to right and left just to be certain. Then he focused his mind on a white blaze in the trunk of an oak tree a dozen yards or so past the man he was going to kill. He started forward, his pace moderate, even, the Crain knife rotating in his fingers into a dagger hold, edge inward.

Five yards.

Three.

Holden lunged forward, his left hand cupping over the mouth and nose, then hauling upward and back as his right arm arced toward the chest and his right fist hammered the Defender down and into the chest where the heart should be.

Death was instantaneous, the body of the man sagging back into Holden's arms and against his chest, emitting a foul odor as muscles relaxed too quickly, a gurgling sound as the fecal material came. Holden eased the dead man to the ground, tearing the knife free. He wiped the blood from it across the man's BDU front, then returned the Defender to its sheath as he looked around him. So far so good, Holden thought.

In the next moment Holden had the rifle, a garden-variety M-16 if ever there was one. As he crouched beside the dead man and popped the magazine, he guessed from the weight of it that the magazine was half full, a thirty to start out with. Two more magazines, fully loaded, were on the man's body; a third was empty.

Holden revised his earlier assessment. It wasn't a training mission these FLNAers had been on but a raid. Inadvertently the infiltration route Holden had picked for his men was a route used by the FLNA forces based at the horse farm, likely a means of reaching the highway where trucks would pass at prearranged times and pick them up, a means of further disguising the horse farm's true purpose.

Holden put one of the fresh magazines up the well of the M-16 and pocketed the full and partially loaded spares in his trousers.

He moved deeper into the enemy position, the M-16 in his right fist, the full-size Beretta in his left.

Whoever the FLNA leader was, he was starting to rally his men forward, closer to the overlook above the ravine. This was clear from the shouted commands, the subtle movement in the trees ahead of him.

Holden kept moving.

In an out-of-place stand of birches, Holden saw his first clear target, two men walking side by side, as if staying close together for protection.

Holden swung the M-16's muzzle toward them and fired, a three-round burst, then another and another. As one of the two, already hit and starting to fall, brought his rifle up to fire, Holden pumped two rounds from the Beretta into the FLNAer's forehead.

He safed the Beretta to get the hammer down and rammed it into his belt as he ran toward the two men. The pattern of gunfire was already changing.

Holden grabbed up one of the M-16s, slung it across his back, then scrounged two more spare magazines. He took up the other M-16, hefting it in his left fist. It was nearly fully loaded.

Holden advanced.

A burst of assault rifle fire came from his left, and the birch beside him lost a chunk of bark. Holden stepped back and wheeled left, both M-16s firing, then again. Gunfire ahead. Holden tucked behind the tree for the little cover it afforded, fired the M-16 from his left hand, fired it again. He dodged right, deeper into the stand, firing two ragged bursts.

Gunfire tore into the trees around him, and Holden threw himself down, rolled down along the contour of the ground, half body slamming into an evergreen. He was up, on his feet, running, gunfire tearing into the trees on both sides of him.

He was near the overlook above the ravine. There was enemy personnel on both sides, and the weapons in both his fists sprayed empty.

A man charged at him from the tree cover on his right, and Holden rammed the M-16 forward, stabbing the flash hider into the FLNAer's left eye, causing a scream so hideous it made Holden's flesh crawl. Holden hit the ground in a roll, while FLNA gunfire from his left cut into two FLNAers coming at him from the right.

The M-16 gone from Holden's right fist, he shifted hands, dumped the magazine from the second rifle, loaded a fresh spare up the well, and sprayed it into the tree cover.

Gunfire was coming from below him, from the direction of the ravine. Holden kept low as he started along the ravine's edge.

Three FLNAers, guns blazing, were rising out of the tree cover. Holden fired, threw himself down, rolled, fired again, then again and again. Two men down. The third man's last burst sprayed up dirt, and Holden's face took the spray, his eyes shutting involuntarily against it. He fired back blindly, spraying the M-16 right and left until it was empty, his eyes barely able to open. The M-16 in his right fist, Holden threw himself down over the edge of the ravine. There was a blur of motion from his left; it was one of the FLNAers tackling him, going over with him.

Holden hit the side of the ravine and rolled. His right knee slammed against something that felt like a rock. Skin was gouged from his left elbow. Locked together with the man who'd thrown himself after him, Holden skidded into the water now. His face went under; his forehead hit a rock.

Holden shook his head as he pulled his face from the water, coughing and choking. The debris that had assailed his eyes was apparently gone. A fist slammed into the side of his face, and Holden's body reacted automatically: His left hand punched forward into the FLNAer's throat; his right hand grabbed a handful of greasy, wet hair. Holden, on his knees in the stream bed, threw his upper body weight forward, his left hip pushing outward, his legs working him upward, his right hand dragging the FLNAer by the head. He pitched the man forward into the water.

For the first time Holden actually saw the man, who was well over six feet, heavily muscled, and beer-potted.

But for all his size, the man was fast. The FLNAer's right hand filled with a .45 automatic as he rose from the water. Holden threw himself forward; his left hand found the FLNAer's gun hand, and the hammer fell on the web of Holden's hand instead of on the firing pin. Holden's body mass hurtled the man down; flesh tore as Holden's fist closed over the gun, twisted it away. Holden's right knee smashed up, missing the crotch, impacting the abdomen. A rush of bad breath washed over Holden's face and throat. Holden's right fist hammered forward, smashing the FLNAer's nose sideways.

At last the man released his grip on the .45, and Holden tore his hand free, shook the gun away from his flesh, reached for it with his right hand as it started to fall, blood spurting from the web of his left hand. But a knee smash impacted him in the right hip, and he skidded away, the gun crashing down into the water. As Holden spread-eagled into the stream, the FLNAer was on him, Holden's arms pinned under him by the tremendous weight.

Blows rained down on Holden's head and neck and back; his consciousness started to ebb.

The fingers of Holden's left hand edged upward, to the pouch on his belt for the Leatherman Tool. It was only a tool, not a weapon, not intended as one. One-handed, Holden forced it open, his fingers nearly numbing and releasing it as a fist or knee smashed against his left shoulder blade.

The tool was open, and he pried the handles apart, exposing the pliers. Holden stabbed it back, found flesh, then squeezed.

There was an animal-like scream, and the pressure on the left side of Holden's body eased. Holden's left hand let go of the pliers, and he snapped his left elbow up and back, contacting bone. His left arm numbed with the blow, but the man rolled off his back.

Holden staggered to his knees, half fell, then mule-kicked the man in the face with his left foot.

The .45—the FLNAer was going for it. Holden reached to his left side. There was no time to find out whether or not he'd lost the full-size Beretta in the fight. His fist closed on the butt of the Beretta Compact instead, and he ripped it from the leather.

The water beside his head exploded as the FLNAer's .45 discharged. Holden punched the 9mm forward and fired twice, then twice again, then twice more. The FLNAer's neck and face splotched red; his eyes rolled wide, the .45 fell from his fist as it opened; the body toppled back. Holden fired twice more. The body twitched as it fell down.

Holden rolled over into the water, which washed across his face. He spit it away as he pushed himself back to his knees and looked toward the dead man. He found the military Beretta still in his trouser band.

Men stared down from the overlook of the ravine.

Holden waited for the gunfire to start.

But they moved back from the edge.

He heard Patsy Alfredi shouting to him, "David!"

"Hold your fire."

The FLNAers were moving back, the muzzles of their weapons lowering.

And Holden looked again at the man in the water.

He had been their leader.

Holden bent to the water to retrieve his pliers.

# CHAPTER
# 15

The two men at the counter were getting up to leave. Rose Shepherd was drinking her third cup of coffee, had barely touched the food. It would have been nice to get up and go to the bathroom. Truck stop rest rooms were usually moderately clean. But calling attention to herself by leaving the booth she occupied might be the wrong move. She often thought that female cops developed better bladder control than women in other jobs. When you sat stakeout duty, there wasn't usually time to find a powder room.

Now Rose Shepherd noticed something she hadn't noticed before: As the man named Johnson walked toward the cash register, he limped. And something clicked for her. In the shooting involving the two FBI agents weeks before, the gunman, who had escaped, had been wounded. There had been signs of heavy bleeding near the scene, according to one of the Patriot informants on Metro PD.

They paid their bill at the cash register, the pink-uniformed woman who had waited on her taking the money. Johnson bought a package of cigarettes, the acne-faced kid with him buying chewing gum.

And Johnson and his Leopard friend left.

Rose Shepherd realized she had been holding her breath, and she let it go. There were many disadvantages to being a woman cop, but one decided advantage was invisibility. A male subject looked, maybe, if you were pretty, but unless he was on the make, that was the end of it. Just another woman, not a threat. Although a significant and growing number of women were police officers, people expected police officers to be male.

Rose Shepherd's eyes followed Johnson and the Leopard as they crossed the parking lot. Her stomach knotted for an instant as the two rent-a-cops crossed Johnson and the Leopard's path, gave them a friendly wave and a smile. "Assholes," Rose Shepherd hissed under her breath.

She opened her purse, quickly took out her wallet, opened the coin-purse side, and found some quarters, which she put on the table under the edge of her saucer. As she stood, she closed the button just above the waistband of her skirt, then picked up the guest check. Her purse over her right shoulder now, the sweater across her shoulders again, she walked to the cash register.

The bill went on the counter, and she started to fish out a ten from her wallet.

"Don't have thirteen cents, honey, do ya?"

Rose Shepherd looked quickly toward the parking lot. Johnson and the Leopard were standing beside a green Chevrolet. "Yes, here." She put a dime and three pennies on the counter and got back paper money from her ten, folded it into her wallet, dropped the wallet into her purse. She kept her right hand inside the bag as she started for the door, her fist closing on the butt of her .45.

Her cop instincts told her that if she tried anything with Johnson and the acne-faced Leopard with him, they'd be armed, the two rent-a-cops would butt in, and she'd be in the middle of a three-sided gun battle. Experience told her that the best bet was to follow them. But David was expecting that she'd be here, waiting for him.

The Leopard was starting to get into the Chevrolet, and as he started through the door, a gun fell out of the waistband of his blue jeans under his windbreaker and hit the pavement. He reached for it just as the two security guards were looking toward the Chevrolet, almost as if fate had planned it.

The two rent-a-cops resolved Rose Shepherd's dilemma.

"Hey, boy!" The fatter one made the shout.

The Leopard froze for an instant, his hand inches away from his gun, some kind of autoloader she couldn't identify at the distance.

Rose started pulling the Detonics Servicemaster from her purse, simultaneously jacking the hammer back to full stand with her thumb. As her gun cleared the bag, the rent-a-cops were starting to go for their guns.

Johnson (or whoever he really was) opened fire. Where the submachine gun had come from, she wasn't certain, maybe from the front seat under a raincoat or blanket.

The fat security guard's body rocked back as though he had been hit by a truck. Rose Shepherd dodged left, the .45 clear now, coming into both fists in a point shoulder position. The other rent-a-cop had his revolver out.

Simultaneously the Leopard and Johnson fired toward him.

Rose Shepherd fired, too. Her first round was low, but the distance was seventy-five yards. Still, the bullet skated across the hood of the Chevrolet and made sparks, shattering the driver's side mirror. Her second bullet hit the windshield, and whether it punched through or not, she couldn't see, didn't have the time to worry.

The second rent-a-cop wheeled toward her, almost losing his balance from the way he seemed to catch for a second, fired his revolver, then fired again. The glass of the truck stop window behind her shattered as he kept firing. A scream came from inside the diner.

There was a telephone booth, one of the old-style ones like those Superman used to change in, and she dived for it. Beside where she landed was a puddle of motor oil or something worse, and the stuff, whatever it was, smeared across the left side of her skirt. She fired past the security guard, toward Johnson and the submachine gun.

The guard just stood there, in the open, fumblingly trying to reload his six-shot revolver.

"Get down! Get down!" she screamed so loudly at him that her throat hurt.

The submachine gun opened up again as Rose Shepherd fired the last two shots in her pistol. She was going for a different target this time, for the Leopard running toward the rent-a-cop, his pistol firing fast. Rose Shepherd was already making a tactical magazine change to one of the eight-round Detonics spares from her purse as the Leopard spilled forward, his legs swept out from under him.

She glanced toward the rent-a-cop. But he was down dead, too.

Submachine-gun fire ripped through the telephone booth, neat three-round bursts; the glass in the booth shattered, spraying her hair and her clothes.

There was another scream from inside the diner.

Her right thumb downed the slide release, and she stabbed the pistol toward Johnson, her eyes squinting against the rain of glass shards. She fired, moving the muzzle right and left, up and down, trying for a random hit, the best she could hope for.

The submachine gun stopped firing as she rammed her last fully loaded magazine up the butt of the Commander-size Detonics, working the slide release.

The green Chevrolet was moving, the passenger-side door still open, Johnson cutting a wide arc across the parking lot. She could hear sirens in the distance. They sounded like state police.

Johnson thrust the submachine gun out the driver's-side window, firing. More glass behind her shattered. She heard more screaming.

Rose Shepherd stood up, the phone booth's meager cover gone, her pistol at the maximum extension of her arms as she fired. Then again and again and again and again and again, she fired it out as the Chevrolet swerved away from her. The submachine gun fell through the open window. She'd hit him, she told herself.

The Chevrolet bounced on a speed breaker, swerved, recovered, and headed for the driveway.

She stuffed the Detonics into the waistband of her skirt, tore open the bottom button of her blouse, reached for the Smith & Wesson Model 60, and pulled it from the Null holster beside her left breast. She wasn't stupid and would have had to have been to try a two-inch snubby revolver against a moving car better than 150 yards away.

She wheeled toward the diner, the revolver bunched tight in her right fist. Some of the truckers were coming outside, stepping through the shot-out glass doors. "Be cool, guys! Call an ambulance for those two." And she nodded toward the fallen security guards. But she knew they were past needing an ambulance except for transportation to the morgue.

The truckers kept their distance. As she edged away, toward the Ford, she shouted to them, "Those guys were FLNA. If you saw the gunfight, you know who opened up first, you know who killed the two rent-a-cops. So tell it that way!"

Rose Shepherd shifted the revolver into her left hand, her right hand digging in the pocket of her skirt as she ran for the car. She retrieved the keys, stabbed the right one into the lock, slipped behind the wheel, stabbed the squared key into the ignition, and threw her revolver onto the seat. She stomped the gas pedal as she threw the transmission into drive and peeled out like some kid on Saturday night with one too many beers in him, the door slamming as she cut the wheel in a hard right.

The truckers weren't chasing after her. But some of them were huddled over the two rent-a-cops.

"Shit!" Rose Shepherd snarled.

But she had wounded Johnson, she told herself. And she'd gotten the license plate number, instinctively memorizing it as the Chevrolet had sped out of the parking lot.

The state police sirens were louder now. Rose Shepherd slowed a little at the cut for the driveway, then turned right, onto the U.S. highway and away from the interstate, the most likely approach route for the state police or any county cops.

She looked down at her clothes. The blue skirt was smeared with black goo. In her haste to get at her revolver, she had torn the buttonhole on her blouse and the button was lost somewhere. Her white sweater was gone.

But what irritated her most was that she felt like crying.

"Shit!"

She kept driving and held back the tears.

# CHAPTER
## 16

It was a matter of elementary caution. Before borrowing
Patsy Alfredi's Dodge van so he could drive to the diner
in order to rendezvous with Rose, David Holden had
checked with Mitch Diamond to see if with Mitch's powerful base station setup, it would be possible to sort
through police calls. There would be plenty of them,
Holden knew, the gunfire in the woods attracting sirens
before he and the Patriots were even clear of the area, but
not so quickly that there had been any difficulties getting
away. Several of the Patriots had sustained minor
wounds of various kinds; but almost miraculously, none
of the wounds appeared to be life-threatening, and there
had been no fatalities.

"David, we've got problems. Over."

"Talk to me, Mitch." They were using two sidebands
which it was unlikely would be monitored simultaneously, and specially designed boosters had been added to
their CB radios to strengthen the signals which ordinary
citizens band equipment would have picked up as weak
and garbled.

"That diner up by the interstate. There was a gunfight

there, too; three dead." David Holden almost dropped
the microphone from his hand. It was full daylight now
and hot in the pine woods, but he shivered anyway. "All
males. There was a report of a woman who matches
Rosie's description fleeing the scene after the fight. No
report that she was injured or anything. But that's not
the bad part. Been pickin' up really suspicious stuff that
points to some sort of large-scale police raid. Could have
hit our base camp. Over."

Holden's few options were clear. Holden dispatched
Patsy Alfredi and three others toward the interstate to
pick up whatever intelligence might be available concerning the shoot-out at the diner in the event that such information might prove necessary for locating Rose Shepherd. He divided the remainder of his force into two
units, taking seven with him ahead toward the base camp
in order to confirm or deny the information Mitch had
passed along, to cut off Rosie Shepherd should she go
there, her logical course of action, or, if she had already
reached the site and there was trouble at the camp, to get
her out of it. The rest of the Patriot members Holden sent
ahead to an alternate location in company with the
wounded. That location had fewer amenities but was possibly much safer under the circumstances.

As they drove, Holden changed into the battle gear his
people had brought for him preparatory to the now-
aborted assault on the horse farm being used as an FLNA
base. And the Metro Patriots were that now, he realized:
his people, his unit, no longer a group of men and women
whose leadership he had merely assumed to fill the vac-
uum left by the death of Rufus Burroughs.

Rufus Burroughs. As he strapped the Southwind Sanctions SAS-style holster to his right thigh, the Desert Eagle .44 Magnum already in place, he thought of the man

whose pistol the Desert Eagle had been. And for the hundredth or thousandth or ten thousandth time, David Holden asked himself, If he had heeded Burrough's warnings earlier, would Elizabeth and the children still be alive? It was a question which would remain unanswered for as long as he lived.

The van rambled across the rutted ranch road as Holden slipped forward and settled into the front passenger seat. "Pass me my rifle, Pete," he told Pedro Villalobos. Villalobos nodded and handed across the M-16, butt first. Mechanically Holden checked the Colt assault rifle's condition of readiness.

"You wanna stop near that rise, David. We're there," Helen Swensen announced, pointing through the tinted glass of the windshield toward a loaf-shaped upthrust of gray granite.

As Holden looked up from his weapon, he gestured to their right, toward a stand of out-of-flower dogwoods and wild water oaks. "Pull in over there, Helen."

Yellow sunlight shone down in strong, dust-mote-filled shafts between the branches of towering pecan trees and live oaks. As the van eased beneath the forest canopy, Holden threw open the front passenger door. He climbed out the moment the vehicle stopped as the van still rocked on its springs. Beyond where the diagonal bands of light penetrated, the woods were cloaked in smoky shadow. Holden squinted against the light, his BDUs sticking to him almost instantly with sweat; despite the early-morning hour, it was already insufferably hot and the van's air conditioning made the air temperature seem that much worse by contrast.

Holden slung the M-16 diagonally, muzzle downward, across his back.

The side door slid open, and the six men along with

Helen Swensen dispersed into the trees as planned. Holden started for the rise. It was weathered rough in spots, smooth in others, but weeks earlier he had climbed it to determine if it would make a suitable observation post, and he was confident he could get up along the rock's treacherous surface again without breaking his neck. At least he hoped he could.

It was slow going and a diagonal traverse much of the time, only protracting the time involved. With no more than a moderately serious slip, which cost some skin from his right wrist, Holden reached the top, then edged forward and upward slightly on his knees and elbows, the granite hot as metal in the sunlight. At the lip of the overlook Holden stopped. He reached to his side for the field glasses he'd taken from the van, raised the $8 \times 30$s, and adjusted their focus.

In the distance, with sickening clarity, he could see the ruins of their camp, police vehicles and ambulances surrounding the ragtag collection of pop-up campers and tents and the farmhouse proper. Weapons, ammunition, medical supplies, food, clothing, and people all gone.

The money and pistol his father-in-law had left in the safety-deposit box, the family photos of his dead wife and his three dead children Holden had, wisely, he now knew, buried in a hermetically sealed plastic survival canister, the location of which was known only to Rosie Shepherd and himself. It was at the moment of burying it, sharing that secret with her, that he had first realized the depth of the feelings he had for her.

There were black rubberized body bags ranked between the farmhouse and the ambulances, black-uniformed Metro SWAT officers strutting about with automatic weapons.

"God damn you," David Holden muttered.

But he was at once relieved and puzzled. There was no sign of Rosie Shepherd. . . .

The hem of Rose Shepherd's already ruined skirt caught in the thorns of a pale green vine trailer, and she stopped to tug the fabric free. It was then that she heard the voices in the woods just ahead of her, unfamiliar voices, sounding brash and at once a little nervous, too.

As quietly as she could, she freed her clothing, bunching the skirt around her legs, and crouched there, listening. There had been no extra ammo in the Ford as a precaution against a roadside search. The police had to be really suspicious to try a body search or be acting on a tip. Usually they contented themselves with searching trunks and glove compartments and long, meaningful looks to the backseat and the floor.

All she had to defend herself, except for her knife, was the little snubby .38 Special Chiefs and an extra five rounds in the solitary speed loader she habitually carried for it. Her tiny right fist was sweating on the revolver's butt.

She could hear the voices quite distinctly now. ". . . aren't no more a them 'round here."

"Look, man, Kaminsky says 'Get out there in the woods and look for more Patriots,' so we get out in the woods and look for more damn Patriots. Big fuckin' deal. We walk around a little, then get on the old Motorola and tell 'im all the Patriots is gone, right?"

"Shouldn't a been doin' shit with these Patriots. It's the FLNA bastards we oughta be nailin'."

"Then you go tell that one to Kaminsky, boy."

She could see them now, both of them in black SWAT gear, so young they looked barely old enough to be out of school, carrying their M-16 rifles by the handles like attaché cases. It would take precious seconds of fumbling to bring the rifles into any sort of shooting position unless these men were very good, and had they been very good, the rifles would not have been carried that way in the first place. One of the men seemed, at most, only negligibly taller than she, Rose Shepherd decided. And both of them stood with their backs toward her now, fewer than six feet away on the other side of the natural hedge of honeysuckle. The Motorola they had spoken of would be set to receive, not to send. With the rifles carried in their right hands and both men wearing their pistols in strong side carries, it would be just as awkward for them to get to their handguns as to use the rifles.

Once, for Halloween, when she was just a teenager, she had dressed up like Daniel Boone with a broomstick flint-lock rifle and her hair stuffed out of sight under a Davy Crockett hat she'd found at a garage sale. Rose Shepherd felt the corners of her mouth set into a smile.

She raised herself to her full height and pointed the snubby .38 Special right at the air space separating the backs of their heads. "Touch your guns and you're dead. And Happy Halloween." No coonskin caps were available, but there were two black baseball caps with brassards in front reading METRO SWAT.

After David Holden had reconnoitered from the height of the rise, he clambered down again, determined that something be done quickly, despite the obvious risks, to free the Patriots whom he saw cuffed and waiting for transport, waiting for interrogation and eventual incarceration. There were stories coming out of some of the other large metropolitan areas that captured Patriots were being held—however illegally—"for the duration," and how long that might be no one could guess at this stage. There were other stories that were even worse, stories concerning drug therapy to loosen tongues. It was hard for him to accept that American police officers would do such things, harder still now after his meeting with Rudolph Cerillia and the trust he had begun to feel for Luther Steel to believe that the FBI would condone such procedures. If something were to be done to free the captured Patriots, it had to be done immediately. Trucks from the television newspeople, even a helicopter from one of the stations, were already on site, and there seemed to be no sign that whoever had led the raid was about to whisk the Patriot prisoners away before milking all the publicity possible out of them. That was to the good. But there were two police choppers as well, both of them large enough to carry a dozen men or more if passenger comfort and fuel economy weren't a serious concern.

Part of the very specialized SEAL training he had been given years ago had included the opportunity to learn to fly fixed-wing single-engine aircraft and military helicopters. But that has been more years ago than he wanted to consider. As a university professor he had had the money to keep up with flying. The additional money he had earned with his illustrations for science-fiction short stories or the occasional cover art assignment had never been "extra" money, merely used to provide the family with a little something over the bare necessities. There had been times, as a reservist, when he had flown as the guest of someone in a base flying club, but that flying had always been fixed-wing.

Pete Villalobos, on the other hand, had been a medevac pilot in Vietnam. Pete was quiet, a loner, like most of the men David Holden had met who had shared that MOS during the Vietnam War and lived to come home. There was probably ample reason for his silence. If war were hell, then the medevac pilots had found something worse than hell.

Pete and Helen and the other five Patriots who had accompanied Holden were clustered around him now. He had signaled them back after finishing his reconnaissance. "Here's what we're going to do." And he looked at Pedro Villalobos. "Can you still fly a chopper?"

"Yes. One of those?"

"Yeah."

"Yes."

"Then we've got a chance," Holden rasped. . . .

* * *

For once in her life Rose Shepherd wished that she were flat-chested. With the liberated equipment slung properly to her body—the strap for the gas mask bag and the strap for the magazine carrier crossing her front—her breasts were only accentuated despite the loose fit of the black BDU top. And there were no female SWAT officers, something she had protested against vigorously and often before her abrupt separation from Metro PD when she had seen Rufus Burroughs walking out with a drawn gun on Ralph Kaminsky.

Using the Cold Steel Mini-Tanto, rather than one of the fantasy fighting knives the SWAT guys had carried, she had directed the larger of the two men to cut his pants and top into strips, then bind the smaller man with the strips, gagging him as well, and bind his own ankles and gag himself. With her revolver to his head, she had (awkwardly but effectively) bound the larger man's wrists. Once both men had been secured, she had double-checked every knot and tightened the gags. Then she blindfolded them. It was a terrible thing to do to men whom only months before she would have called brother officers regardless of their apparent ineptitude, but she had no choice. The Patriots' camp was compromised, some of her new "brothers and sisters" were prisoners, and there was no telling when David and the others would arrive to help.

With the two SWAT cops blindfolded, she didn't feel quite so brazen undressing down to her underpants and bra, but she didn't feel exactly comfortable either. She made no attempt to salvage the skirt and blouse, both ruined; but the slip was still perfectly good, and she stuffed that inside her BDU top. Even the smaller man's combat boots were ridiculously large for her, but they

would have to do. She was able to secure her own shoes
and her purse inside the gas mask bag, discarding the
mask, hoping that wouldn't prove to be a mistake.

Rose Shepherd looked away from the mirror by which
she had been applying camouflage stick thoughtfully pro-
vided by one of the SWAT cops. She looked at the help-
lessly bound men, then stuffed her hair beneath the baseball cap. "Sorry, guys." With the confiscated rifles and
handguns, she started toward the camp. About fifty yards
from where she'd left the two men, she shoved one of the
M-16s under some brush. The pistols both men carried
were Glock 17s, excellent 9mms. One of these she left
holstered; the other she secured under her BDU blouse
beside her bunched-up slip.

As she walked, she reached to the bellows pocket on
her left thigh and took out her cigarettes and lighter,
both of which she had transferred from her purse. She lit
a cigarette now, intentionally letting it hang from the left
corner of her mouth. Her left eye squinted a little against
the upward-wafting smoke, but anything that would
make her appear less feminine was worth a try.

She kept walking, seeing a knot of SWAT-uniformed
officers in the distance, but not seeing O'Brien, the Metro
SWAT commander. They were beside one of the black
SWAT vans and there was a blond woman reporter talking with them. "Shit." Rose Shepherd turned off right,
aiming toward the farmhouse where the prisoners—her
friends—were being forced to stand.

She neared the house, her gloved right fist tight on the
grip of the M-16. And Rose Shepherd almost froze in her
tracks because she saw Ralph Kaminsky.

# CHAPTER
# 18

Luther Steel's body streamed sweat.

Living alone as he had since accepting the assignment to lead the special task force and being separated from his wife and children, he had developed a rather regimented way of life.

When the alarm rang, he jumped out of bed immediately because there was no one to awaken him after "just another couple of minutes, baby," and he had never trusted snooze alarms. After answering nature and while his water heated for instant decaffeinated coffee, he took a quick shave. He had coffee, juice, toast, and a vitamin pill and then a quick workout. He had found bodybuilding the perfect conditioning for a man on a tight, sometimes inflexible schedule, and he practiced it religiously. When time allowed, he did a routine each evening as well. If anything, he was more fit than ever.

He turned on the shower just as he heard the telephone ring. "Shit." He turned off the water, almost slipped stepping over the side of the tub, dripped water as he exited the bathroom and walked across the living room of his apartment, and caught the phone on the fourth ring.

He'd gotten a late start after being up all hours with Rudolph Cerillia and Holden and Detective Shepherd and a more detailed meeting with Mr. Cerillia afterward. Cerillia himself insisted, "Sleep in this morning, Luther; you look like you could use it."

There had been no evening workout. Just shrugging out of his clothes and falling into bed had been an effort.

"This is Steel."

It was Clark Pietrowski; the old guy was as tough as he looked. "You just up?"

"Why?"

"Didn't turn on the tube, did ya?"

"Why?"

"That asshole Kaminsky raided the Patriots' base camp; killed some, took some prisoners, and is gonna hold a damn news conference on the scene, live, in about" —Pietrowski was apparently consulting his watch —"about ten minutes."

"That moron."

"You always have a kind word to say for somebody, Luther."

"Pick me up—five or six minutes."

"Should I maybe bring something special?"

"Bring Tom LeFleur and Bill Runningdeer. Shit!" He slammed down the receiver and walked quickly back toward the bathroom. He always planned his time so he could take a long shower. As he stepped under the water, still adjusting it with one hand and rubbing shampoo into his hair with the other hand, he remembered the old Robert Burns line about "best laid schemes." As he got the water right, he was already washing out the first shot of shampoo.

What if Ralph Kaminsky had busted David Holden? Holden was a man whose discretion could be trusted, but not if he thought the whole thing with Director Cerillia was part of a setup for the raid on the camp. If Holden thought that, he would have to be a fool to keep silent about the meeting last night. And what if Holden had gotten himself killed?

Steel rinsed out the second shampooing, already lathering his chest and abdomen.

And as Steel began to wash the lower portion of his body, he was reminded of Ralph Kaminsky. "What an asshole!"

# CHAPTER
# 19

Rose Shepherd stood beside one of the news vans, watching the television set through the open door, but so close to Ralph Kaminsky that she could see his face as clearly as in person.

His "news conference" was in full sway.

". . . these people. It is well to remember that no man is above the law, no man can take the law into his own hands. That is what the Patriots attempt to do every day. But no more. Not in Metro. Under my leadership this raid has broken the back of the Patriot cell operating in and around Metro. And at last we can devote full resources to the problem posed by the Front for the Liberation of North America. While these so-called Patriots were at large, provoking the FLNA to violence, all hope of bringing about a peaceful and equitable settlement with the FLNA was gone.

"But not anymore," Kaminsky continued. He had pinned on a Beretta and a flak vest and baseball cap, but he looked even more stupid than he usually did. "And I want to serve warning to anyone listening out there who might harbor sympathies for these lawless men and women captured here today." He gestured toward her friends, restrained with disposable plastic cuffs, ranked behind him, SWAT personnel flanking them on either side just out of camera with automatic weapons leveled. "What has happened to these people can happen to you if you are so stupid as to think that you have some God-given right to violate the law. No one has that right."

Around the camp she judged there were at least three dozen SWAT personnel, all of them armed with various semiautomatic pistols and, except for the few with submachine guns, all of them armed with M-16s. Though some of the Patriots standing behind Kaminsky were wounded, all seemed able to move. Medical personnel attended the more seriously wounded on the far side of the farmhouse's front porch. On the lawn before the near side of the porch were the body bags.

Her eyes came back to the screen. The camera panned the display of weapons laid out on the farmhouse kitchen table and on the ground on both sides and in front of it. Kaminsky still blabbered on. Most of the weapons were handguns and conventional rifles and shotguns. There were a dozen or so M-16s, originally liberated from the FLNA after the FLNA had stolen them from government armories. Most of the crates of ammunition, she knew, were empty of ammunition and had canned goods stored in them. The explosives and LAWS rockets were something she had never seen at the farmhouse before, and she realized Kaminsky had probably brought them to use as window dressing for his news conference.

The few submachine guns that also had been taken during raids against the FLNA were Uzis, probably smuggled into the country by FLNA fellow travelers, their origins most likely stolen or rerouted third world arms shipments. None of the FLNA weapons ever checked by Metro PD had any legitimate purchase record, and she doubted the case was any different anywhere else in the United States.

As she stared at Ralph Kaminsky on the television, Rose Shepherd made a decision. David would have labeled it irrational and been furious with her for trying it. But Rose Shepherd smiled to herself, knowing that David would have tried it, too.

Where was David?

The gunfire he'd gone to answer?

She forced the thoughts of death and disaster from her mind as she walked away from the news van. Without David— She shivered and forced away that thought, too. She had never had love in her life, not the kind of love that there was between a man and a woman, not the kind of love she felt for David Holden. Rose Shepherd had checked the condition of readiness on all her borrowed ordnance, including the Glock 17 under her BDUs, checked everything before she approached the farmhouse. She was as ready as she would ever be. . . .

David Holden reached the far edge of the field of fescue grass, being grown, he knew, as feed for livestock. There were all the helicopters, the two marked for Metro PD and the television station helicopter as well, this last some sort of Bell Ranger. The fescue was knee-high, and as Holden dropped into it to work his way forward on knees and elbows, he felt reasonably confident that its height would obscure his movements at least from casual observation.

Three men stood at the rough center between the machines. Two were in police uniforms, and the remaining one was in stylish-looking civvies that seemed more appropriate attire for a yachtsman than a pilot. Holden kept

moving, hearing the telltale sounds of Pete Villalobos
moving off to his left.

Holden, as all of them worked their way toward their
positions, had decided on something. Rather than trust to
his long rusted skills with a helicopter, he would impress
into service one of the pilots. As for the third helicopter,
it could easily be disabled.

Holden kept moving.

Fifty yards now to the nearest of the choppers, the one
belonging to the news station.

Forty yards.

Thirty.

Twenty-five.

Holden peered out along the swaying tops of the blades
of grass. The three pilots were still preoccupied.

Again Holden kneed and elbowed his way forward, the
M-16 strapped tight across his back, the Defender knife
in his right fist.

He reached the shadow made by the news helicopter,
sweat drying on him almost instantly as he left the blazing glare of the sun, the contrast in ambient temperature
so pronounced that he shivered. He glanced to his left as
he rose out of the grass into a crouch. Villalobos gave
him a thumbs-up sign. Holden raced toward the chopper.

Knowing how to sabotage a helicopter was stock-in-
trade for David Holden in his SEAL team days, and he
sabotaged this one both quickly and obviously, obviously
enough that no one could get it airborne without realiz-
ing the craft was disabled. As Holden left the machine,
he sheathed the Crain knife and drew the Desert Eagle
from the Southwind Sanctions holster at his right thigh.

He could see Villalobos clearly, already in position beside the nearer of the police helicopters.

As his and Villalobos's eyes met, Villalobos nodded, settling his M-16 toward the three pilots.

Holden stepped away from the fuselage of the television station's chopper and thumbed back the hammer of the Desert Eagle. "Yo! Guys!" The two police officers turned, starting to draw, but Holden shouted toward them, "Freeze or you're dead! You're completely surrounded."

The two policemen hesitated for the fatal second, and the realization that they'd lost was suddenly clear in both their faces. "Pete, come out and get their guns! The rest of you, shoot if they try anything!" Holden kept both men covered with the .44 while Villalobos ran up, the M-16 in his right fist. Both men stepped back with hands raised as Villalobos lifted their service revolvers. "On the ground! Move!" Holden commanded, and all three men dropped to their knees, then to their faces. While Holden kept his gun on them, Villalobos frisked the three; he found no other weapons. "You in the middle," Holden said, "roll over onto your left side. Move it!" The police pilot at the center of the three men obeyed. Villalobos took the man's cuffs and used them to lock the pilot's hands behind him. Then Villalobos took the second police officer, rolled him onto his right side, and, using the second set of cuffs, looped them through the first man's cuffs to bind him. The television station pilot looked up. Holden gestured with the Desert Eagle. "You know what caliber this is?"

"No."

"It's a forty-four Magnum. Ever see any *Dirty Harry* movies?"

"Right."

"Same thing, only it's an auto instead of a revolver. Up."

The pilot got to his feet. Villalobos handed the man a set of keys, saying, "You fly that one; I'll fly this one. Yours doesn't fly anymore."

"Right."

Holden grabbed the pilot by the shoulder and started propelling him toward the police chopper as Villalobos quickly unloaded the police ordnance and pocketed the ammo, then put the guns on the ground. Enough of the Patriots had been cops at one time or another to appreciate the hassles a policeman went through when his gun was stolen. . . .

Rose Shepherd stood fewer than ten feet from Ralph Kaminsky, who was fielding questions from the press and, in general, making himself come off like a combination of Eliot Ness and George Patton, with a slight Kennedyesque flavor and a smile most reminiscent of Herman Munster.

As Kaminsky was answering a question about the true motivation of the "so-called Patriots who use the current crisis as a cover for vigilantism," Rose Shepherd brought the Glock out from under her BDU top, shoved the blond female reporter down on her butt as she moved forward in three steps, and stood beside Ralph Kaminsky, the muzzle of the 9mm going to his nose. "Ralphie, baby, don't let anybody do anything rash."

Ralph Kaminsky's eyes widened, and his jaw dropped. Bolts of automatic weapons were racked all around her. If someone lost his head, both she and Ralph Kaminsky would be dead in the next second.

"Ralph, I'd have put this pistol to your head, except you don't have any brains to shoot out. But at least with your nose, there's gotta be something in there."

"Don't! Don't try to stop her!" Kaminsky shouted to the men around them.

Rose Shepherd eyed the crowd, police officers, and newspeople. "Keep the damn cameras rolling!"

Questions were fired at her, and she shrieked over them, "Just shut up and listen!" The reporters quieted, and her borrowed ordnance pressed against Kaminsky's face, Rose Shepherd turned to face the cameras. "All of you out there. I'm Rose Shepherd, a former detective with Metro PD. Ralph Kaminsky has lied to you all. While Kaminsky and people like him waste time and manpower and resources chasing down the Patriots, the FLNA runs out of control. The Patriots were formed to do what the police couldn't or wouldn't do: stop the FLNA while there's still a country left to save. When men like Ralph Kaminsky stop using this crisis as a platform for their own political ambitions and put the welfare of the American people ahead of their own egos, there won't be any more need for the Patriots. We're in existence because without us the damn FLNAers would win. Think. Try to understand." There was movement on the far right edge of her peripheral vision, and she realized she hadn't said what she wanted to say and hadn't said anything really well. "Freeze where you are or Kaminsky gets it!"

The movement stopped.

The blond reporter was back on her feet. "What do you want? What are your demands?"

*Demands?* Rose Shepherd thought. "Do you think I'm some sort of terrorist? You're crazy! Get up here," Rose Shepherd said in the next instant, hearing the blonde murmur something into her microphone about being taken hostage. "Get that knife off Kaminsky's belt—now!"

The woman started fumbling at the sheath, trying to take it from the belt. "Just open the damn snap and take out the knife. Can you handle that?" The woman drew the knife—a bayonet for an M-16—and held it as though it were dirty. "Go back there and cut free the tall man with the bandage on his left temple." That was Larry Perkins, a cool-headed man Rose could rely on. "Do it!"

Rose followed the blonde with her eyes for an instant until she seemed to be starting to do what she was told, then glanced around again, to make certain no one was moving to save Kaminsky. "Please, Detective Shepherd, don't shoot me!" Kaminsky's voice cracked.

"Then don't pull any asshole plays and maybe I won't have to."

"No, nobody'll—"

The voice of O'Brien, the SWAT commander, cut in, booming toward her like thunder. "Shepherd! Throw down that weapon!"

"Bullshit!"

"You'll never make it out of here alive."

"Shut up, O'Brien!" Kaminsky snapped, his voice fear-edged and almost little old lady-like. "Shut up! Do you hear me?"

O'Brien stopped talking. Rose Shepherd didn't believe the sound of her own voice as she spoke. It sounded like a snarl. "You've got an ego that won't quit, O'Brien, but what's a good cop doing with a thing like him?"

O'Brien said nothing.

She heard Larry Perkins's voice. "All cut loose, Rosie!"

Without looking back toward him, she ordered, "Take the lady reporter with you while you rearm. Get everything of value you can carry from the farmhouse—medical supplies especially—and get aboard those vans. Start disarming the police." And she hissed at Kaminsky, "And if anybody doesn't hand over his weapon, guess who gets it, Ralphie?"

She heard the sound of helicopters, so suddenly aware of the machines overhead that she was momentarily disoriented. One of O'Brien's SWAT people moved toward her fast, and Rose Shepherd screamed faster, "One more step, and Kaminsky's history!"

A voice came over the public-address system from one of the choppers now almost directly overhead. "Rosie! This is David. We're in control of the helicopters, and the news helicopter's disabled. We're coming in!"

She didn't know what relieved her more, hearing that they were going to win this time or just hearing David Holden's voice. She promised herself, as she kept the Glock to Kaminsky's face, that she would tell David to hold her for a very long time. . . .

David Holden stepped from the chopper, ducking beneath the rotor blades' downdraft, an M-16 in his right fist. The freed Patriots not directly involved in covering or disarming the SWAT personnel and ordinary police closed around him.

Some of the Patriots began it almost simultaneously, then others joined them, and soon all the Patriots, their meager belongings carried in sacks and old cardboard boxes and backpacks, took up the cheering.

The wounded were the first to be put aboard the helicopters while other Patriots disabled the police radios or busied themselves unloading captured police ordnance, the ordnance, but not the loose ammunition or magazines, to be left behind.

In the end two vans were needed in addition to the helicopters. The disarmed SWAT personnel were used to load the vans with equipment, food, and everything else that could be salvaged from the farmhouse; Patsy Alfredi's family scrapbook; the encyclopedia that served as their only reference and often their only source of recreation; the odds and ends of civilization the outlawed Patriots kept for themselves as a last link to former lives.

The remaining police vehicles were disabled, tires deflated and distributor caps pulled. These latter, along with the ammunition and magazines and knives taken from the police, were left in the SWAT vans after the vehicles were abandoned.

Once the ground transportation was clear of the area, both helicopters took off, one piloted by Pedro Villalobos, the other piloted by the television station chopper pilot under the muzzle of David Holden's Beretta 92-F.

At one point the pilot recruited by force snapped, "You won't shoot me. How will you land?"

"You'll never know," Holden told him in reply.

The pilot said nothing else.

David Holden's other hand, the one not holding the Beretta 9mm, held Rose Shepherd's hands.

# CHAPTER

## 20

Luther Steel flashed his ID and passed the police officer before the man could say anything, Pietrowski, Runningdeer, and LeFleur in a wedge behind him. Tom LeFleur growled, "What the hell happened here?"

Luther Steel didn't care to hazard a guess. There were police cars with flat tires, police vans with flat tires, a half dozen men surrounding a television station helicopter in the field they'd passed by as they drove along the rutted ranch road toward the farmhouse.

Bill Runningdeer said, "If you ask me, these guys got caught with their pants down." And as Luther Steel glanced back at Runningdeer, he followed Runningdeer's eyes toward a man in Metro SWAT black carrying an M-16 without a magazine in it.

"Our newfound friends are pretty good." Clark Pietrowski laughed under his breath.

Beside the front porch of the farmhouse Ralph Kaminsky was holding sway over a group of reporters, and Steel angled away, deciding to wait. But Kaminsky called to him from the porch. "You! Steel! What are you doing here?"

Half the reporters clustered around Kaminsky broke off and ran toward Steel and his team. Steel mentally shrugged, shouted back as he approached the porch, "I understood there were to be some arrests here of various persons wanted in connection with federal warrants." He had to keep Kaminsky off his back about the mess at the hospital, at least in front of the press, so he put the ball back into Kaminsky's court. "Did something go wrong here? Why are all your vehicles down? Why are there men walking around with empty weapons?"

The reporters were firing questions so loudly and so rapidly that Steel understood what it must have been like to be in attendance when the Tower of Babel was completed. His three men formed ranks around him to keep the reporters back as Kaminsky shouted, somehow his annoying voice heard over all of the rest, "I'd like to know, Agent Steel, for the record, just whose side you are on!"

Luther Steel didn't say the first answer that came into his head—it would have been obscene—but he said what he felt. "I'm on the side of the law, sir. I'd like to think that's the cause we both serve. Rather than attempt to confound federal involvement in these matters, I would think you'd be more interested in cooperating in order to bring these matters to a successful resolution. I'm not here for publicity. I'm here to serve the law and, through serving the law, serve the public trust; I hope we share the same intent, sir."

There was a gap in the wall of reporters between them, and Steel could see Kaminsky's face clearly. The jaw dropped wide open, and no words came. The muscles were tight at the edges of his eyes, which were dark with hate.

# CHAPTER

## 21

He slid into the front seat of the Mercedes, his right hand on the Glock 17 as his eyes swept over the backseat, the interior obligingly (and stupidly) illuminated by the dome light. An inherent lack of trust of anyone was an occupational necessity. And the most dangerous persons to be around were passionate amateurs.

"I don't like meeting like this," the man behind the wheel of the Mercedes half whispered.

"And where would you prefer that we meet? Some restaurant where you could be recognized and some reporter might snap a photograph? Use your head, and keep your nerve."

"Look, Johnson—"

"No, you look," Dimitri Borsoi said, his eyes on the night surrounding the car. "All you have to do is keep saying what you are saying to the press, keep doing what you are doing. Leave the election in my hands. Those are not only your orders as well as mine but the only chance you have to win the election. It is sometimes rare when orders make perfect sense; these orders do. If you allow fear to consume you, then the game is up."

"But what if—"

"What? The plan cannot help succeeding."

"What was that gun battle about—"

Borsoi cut him off. "You heard about that on the news. I assume you read very little—"

"Dammit! I don't have to—"

Borsoi reached across the car and had the pistol against the man's neck in under a second. "No, you could be assassinated here and now; it could be blamed on the Patriots; another candidate could step into your slot very easily. If he were not one of our choosing, he could easily be brought around. Very few people have never done anything for which they could be crucified in the press. Like your passion for—"

"Johnson!"

"For children? Hmm? No—" Borsoi leaned back and made his gun disappear. "That lovely collection of books and videotapes and snapshots. Your fingerprints are all over them. And anyway, you really do feel for the cause, hmm?"

"You know I want us to win."

Borsoi smiled toward the night. "With sincerity like that on our side, how can we lose? No, you keep doing what you do, saying what you say, reacting in your own customary way to the events which will begin unfolding tomorrow. And you will win the election. It is impossible that you would not win. Now, was there anything else that was so urgent?"

"Johnson, it's all right for you. Hell, nobody even knows your real name. But if something goes wrong, my God, man, it's my neck."

"If something goes wrong, you will have caused it. And you will never need to worry about anything ever again because I will kill you myself. And I'm very good at what I do."

Borsoi reached up to the dome light and cupped his left palm across it as he opened the door, then tapped the toe of his left foot against the white plastic plunger so it would depress and shut off the dome light as if the door were closed against the plunger.

"But—"

Borsoi didn't want to listen anymore, and he slipped out of the car. The light came on when the pressure of his foot was taken away from the plunger. He slammed the door behind him and moved off into the bushes.

No one walked the public parks anymore, not even in daylight. No one walked at all if he or she could ride. And no one ventured out at night unless necessity demanded it.

Factory production was down because no one would work night shifts. A producer of defense-related electronic components was attempting a much publicized new technique to lure workers back to evening shifts even after hazardous duty incentives for their paychecks had failed. The government contractor was sending out special buses with security guards aboard who would, it was claimed in the press, not only protect the occupants of the buses but also see them to and from their homes, thus allowing them to work in perfect safety.

The plan was neglecting the obvious, which was always the greatest chink in the armor of any enemy. As Borsoi came down off the wooded slope and toward the chain-link fence on the other side of which his car was located, he looked at his watch. In a matter of moments the assaults on the neglected obvious would begin. Even the least talented among the Front for the Liberation of North America was more than capable of carrying out these assaults. The sale of guns and ammunition had been curtailed for some time now, of course, so that those people who had not been armed for self-protection prior to the curtailment were unable to arm themselves for defense of their homes unless they bought on the black market. Borsoi went over the fence, his leg stiff from the old wound. He also felt a flash of sharp pain across his left forearm from the grazing wound he'd sustained during the gunfight at the truck stop. He was almost certain the woman who'd shot him was Detective Shepherd.

As he slid behind the wheel of the Dodge, his thoughts drifted back to their original course before the pain had distracted him. "Damn bitch," Borsoi murmured, giving a last thought to Detective Shepherd.

An abused handgun in some inferior caliber was black-marketed these days for something in excess of $1,000. Good-quality firearms were impossible to come by, and ammunition in the better calibers was selling for as much as $5 a round.

The populace was in effect disarmed, always an important step—that is, except for the Patriots, and the police seemed so obsessed with capturing Patriots that in some ways the very existence of the Patriots made it easier for the FLNA to operate.

As he turned out of the park onto a street with no lights and many loose paving bricks strewn along the course of his headlights, Borsoi glanced again at his watch. The neglected obvious was being taken care of at this very moment.

The "neglected obvious" was the families of those workers tempted back to the night shift by their defense contractor employer through offers of assured personal safety. While the workers rode their secure little buses, selected houses would be invaded, their occupants killed.

Borsoi lit a cigarette.

# CHAPTER
# 22

One of the principal rules for operating inside enemy territory—and, to a large degree, enemy territory was what the United States of America had become for the Patriots—was to have a system of safe houses. The place to which David Holden had sent the rest of the Patriot cell, after the battle in the woods near the horse farm, was just such a place.

There was no house at all in any true sense of the word, but rather a conglomeration of old shacks and metal buildings erected to house penitentiary prisoners used for a public works project some twenty years before.

Although some of the Patriots eagerly accepted the tin-roofed buildings for shelter, a few others, David Holden and Rosie Shepherd among them, erected tents in the open. The air in the old buildings was stiflingly warm, but despite the heat of the day having lingered well into the evening, there was a cool breeze which could be felt at times in the open. Their tent was the size of two army shelter halves with a tarp floor and a double air mattress over that. With the screening in place, mosquitoes and other flying and crawling unpleasantries were of no real concern.

She was stretched out beside him on her stomach, chin resting on the backs of her hands, elbows supporting her head, clad only in a T-shirt and panties. Holden, stripped down to fresh BDU pants, shirtless and barefoot, lay beside her, staring up at the tent ceiling. Using sun showers and well water, Holden and Rosie had been among the first to shower after reaching the new encampment, then had spent the rest of the day securing the area beyond the preliminary precautions, assessing losses to equipment stores, and planning their next hit against the FLNA.

Neither David Holden nor Rosie Shepherd had spoken of the meeting with Rudolph Cerillia and Luther Steel, agreeing with the FBI personnel that the fewer who knew of the "alliance" formed, the better. Many among the Patriots had been so mistreated at the hands of local law enforcement that it would be hard ever to convince them that someone who wore a badge could be trusted; Holden still harbored doubts.

"Whatcha thinking about?"

"Everything," Holden replied.

"Me?"

"I wasn't thinking about you."

Rosie Shepherd's lower lip distended slightly, affecting a pout.

"What I meant," Holden told her, laughing, "was that I was thinking about everything that was, well, like business. The stuff with Steel and Cerillia and like that. That's why I wasn't thinking about you."

"If I'm not business, then what am I?" Rosie asked him. "Pleasure?"

It was one of those conversations that no matter what he said, she would find some way of turning around on him, Holden realized, his left arm curling under her chest, then drawing her toward him, over him. His right hand gently touched her face, her hair. She kissed the tip of his nose, and he drew her down toward him and kissed her hard on the mouth. "Pleasure, it's definitely pleasure," Holden whispered in her ear an instant before he kissed her ear.

"Hmm," she murmured, her fingers playing over his chest, playing in the hair there. "Women are persons, not sex objects, but I'll make you a deal?"

"Yeah? What kind of deal?"

"I'll be your sex object"—she smiled, her cheeks reddening a little—"if you'll be mine."

Holden rolled her over. He was on top of her now, and Rosie's hands were still against his chest. "That's a deal."

"Tell me it's forever, okay? I mean, one of these days we're gonna buy it, just like Rufus. I know that. But lie to me."

"It's forever," Holden whispered, "and it's not a lie." His mouth pressed down hard against hers. Holden felt Rosie's fingertips gently touch his face, his hair. His right hand reached under the T-shirt she wore, and as she arched her back, his fingers undid the hooks and eyes which closed her bra. Then his hand pushed up the T-shirt and the open bra beneath it, the palm of his hand brushing against the nipple of her left breast, feeling the sudden hardness there.

She pressed herself tightly against him, and the heat of her breasts against his chest was like fire.

Her hands worked at the belt of his BDUs and then began to work at the fly. "Damn buttons," she hissed, her breath hot on him but smelling sweet.

Holden helped her with the buttons, then pushed his pants down; her hands were already tugging at his underpants. Once his pants were below his knees, there was no sense bothering with them. He pulled her panties down, leaving them hooked on her left ankle; no sense bothering anymore with the panties either.

Rosie touched him as Holden kissed her, and suddenly Holden was inside her and Rosie was crying a little and holding him more tightly than she had ever held him and Holden told Rosie he loved her. And in that instant, Holden thought, telling her he loved her was like telling her it was forever—true.

# CHAPTER

# 23

The little girl—younger than his children—hadn't just been killed. Someone had put a knife into her abdomen and all but disemboweled her.

"Motherfuckers." Clark Pietrowski gasped as he entered the house. Then he turned away and rushed back out onto the porch.

Steel thought he heard the sounds of vomiting. He knew such sounds with special intimacy because when he first entered the house, he had rushed out as well, thrown up over the porch rail into a raggedly neglected hedge.

One of the Metro medical examiners, a man Luther Steel had been bumping into more and more, said, "It's different when a kid dies, especially like this. I threw up, too. To top it off, I think they sodomized her. The damn FLNA shits—" Then he clapped Steel on the shoulder and returned to his work.

When Steel reentered the house, he intentionally stared at the girl, photographing the impression of her death into his mind so he would never forget what he saw.

Ralph Kaminsky was conspicuous by his absence.

The television—still on, Steel guessed, from the previous night—was hot as he touched the back of his hand to the wood-looking metal cabinet. The fingerprint technicians were through with this portion of the house. A game show was on, but as Steel started to look away, the game show was interrupted by one of the local news anchors, a pretty woman of about forty. The sound wasn't on, but there was no need for it. The station's standard slide used as an intro backup for reports on the latest FLNA activities appeared. Then there was a quick cutaway to video showing the exterior of the house in which Steel now stood, and the body-bagged form of an adult being carried out. Steel had seen the news crew, seen the body bag when he entered the first time. The newspeople were quick, he thought. He had to give them that. The bulletin ended, and regular programming was resumed. The game show contestant, a pudgy-faced white woman, was hugging the host of the show, and lights flashed in the background.

Luther Steel guessed she'd just won.

"Good for you, lady." He turned away from the television just in time to see the bag with the little girl inside being zipped closed. There were chalk-outlined bloodstains all over the carpet where she had been, and the assistant ME was putting something that looked like a human body part into a plastic bag.

Clark Pietrowski stepped into the doorway, visibly recoiling as the body bag was carried past him on a stretcher. "God. There's another one, Luther. About a mile from here. Guy went to work on one of those security buses and came home. I don't have any particulars yet. We'd better boogie, Steel."

It was hard going through life with the last name of Steel because it somehow gave the impression that like steel, one was somehow impervious to almost anything. . . .

Bill Runningdeer and Tom LeFleur were already on the scene of the second murder by the time Luther Steel and Clark Pietrowski arrived. And before they exited the car, there was another call out on the police band to what sounded like a third.

"Don't go in, Luther," LeFleur warned, but Luther Steel walked past him. LeFleur shouted after him, "They gotta pay for this shit, Luther!"

Luther Steel, Clark Pietrowski beside him, mounted the steps. Pale-faced Metro uniform cops stood by the door, one of them holding his stomach. Steel started to show his ID, but someone off to the side of the small house's front porch said something about its being okay, and Steel merely entered.

No crime scene technicians had been here yet.

There were bodies everywhere.

Six of them.

A partially decapitated woman.

There was a dead child on the floor beside her, a boy of about six.

An older woman, her throat slit, was still in a sitting position on a bentwood rocking chair in the corner of the room, blood staining the front of her dress and a strange look almost like a smile in her eyes.

A teenager, a boy, shot to death.

Two preteenage children, girls, maybe twins, Steel thought, because even in death they seemed so much alike. They both were shot, and it looked as if they might have been raped—before or after, he couldn't tell.

And there was a seventh body.

Just a mutt.

Luther Steel bent over the animal and closed its eyes. The eyelids opened again, and Steel shook his head and closed his own eyes. There was a chunk of clothing stuck in one corner of the dog's mouth, perhaps a piece of clothing from one of the FLNA killers. Luther Steel wished that it were a chunk of flesh instead.

# CHAPTER
## 24

There was a Metro radio DJ named Lem Parrish. As a boy, the way the story went—Pietrowski had told it to Steel—Parrish had always wanted to be a G-man, reading everything he could about men like Eliot Ness, Melvin Purvis, J. Edgar Hoover, and watching all the old Jimmy Cagney films—as Pietrowski put it, the "whole nine yards."

One night an off-duty Metro cop Lem Parrish knew was in the neighborhood grocery store, among the last of the old mom-and-pop places to be suffocated by the supermarket chains. The cop was just "chewing the fat," as Clark Pietrowski recounted it, when two just paroled two-time losers with armed robbery MOs entered the store, one of them with a sawed-off shotgun (later found to have been stolen) and the other with a butcher knife. The off-duty cop reacted when the one with the butcher knife started to use it on the throat of a teenage girl who walked in to buy a loaf of bread. When the cop reacted, so did Lem Parrish. The Metro PD man was wounded but recovered fully and returned to duty. Lem Parrish was wounded but lost all the fingers of his left hand.

Because the Metro cop had shot both fleeing felons, and because the one who survived (the one who had slit the teenage girl's throat and killed her) was fired on without being warned to halt, the suspect was released after the state had paid his hospital bills (on condition that his lawyers settle out of court in the civil suit for use of excessive force).

Parrish tried law school but quit after he realized that although a jury might well sympathize with an attorney missing most of a hand it was more likely to be revulsed. And criminal law was the only sort of law in which he had any interest.

Lem Parrish, six feet tall, blond, handsome, and pariahed by fate, turned to broadcasting. Knowing television was out of his reach because of his physical imperfection, he went into radio. After some chatter, some records, some bad jokes, and some personal appearances with his left wrist and what wasn't there hidden in his pocket, Lem Parrish was a success.

Lem Parrish competed successfully against ten-fingered men in everything from charity basketball games to combat shooting.

He was also a Patriot.

And at the close of the meeting between the FBI leadership and the Metro Patriots leadership, David Holden had returned from a pay phone call and announced that Lem Parrish would be their link.

Luther Steel sat at the bar, sipping a beer so he wouldn't look more out of place than he already did, the only black in a white man's pub.

Lem Parrish slid onto the stool beside him. "This isn't the way it's supposed to be."

"I had to do it in person—at least this time," Luther Steel said, trying to keep his lips from moving too notice-

ably, not looking at Parrish except in the behind-the-bar
mirror.

"Once could be enough, man."

"I need to contact—"

"Don't say who."

"And it's gotta be in person."

"After what happened?" Parrish laughed. "Be serious."

"We had nothing to do with that stupid shit."

"If I figured you had, I wouldn't be here. But it's not
that. They're licking their wounds. And they've got
something on the fire anyway."

"I had the worst morning I ever had in my life. I
was—"

"I can imagine," Parrish said, then: "Or maybe I'm
luckier if I can't imagine. It sounded bad enough off the
wire services and over the police radios. What's it got to
do with our mutual friends?"

Steel exhaled hard. "The wire services don't get everything. And neither do the police radios. We got one of the
guys responsible for the murders."

Steel's eyes followed Lem Parrish's face in the mirror,
the eyes going around and the jaw dropping. And then
the bartender came over and asked Parrish if he wanted
the usual, and Parrish only nodded. Parrish lit a cigarette, looked directly at Steel, and said, "FLNA?"

"Yes."

"And he's singing to cop a plea?"

"Yes."

"There's more, isn't there?"

"Yes." Steel shut up as the bartender returned with an
imported beer Steel had always thought tasted like somebody's urine specimen. As the bartender left, Steel said,
"Just tell David this is maybe the one break both of us

needed. This guy we nailed—and we, not the cops, nailed him—is either the most imaginative guy I've ever met or privy to a lot of the inside intelligence on the FLNA. I couldn't trust a phone. And maybe you shouldn't either."

# CHAPTER
# 25

The short-sleeved knit shirt had been too warm before the sun went down, but it was the only way he could carry without being spotted. With the sun down now, he could have pulled on the old bush jacket he'd brought, but then he would only be too warm again.

In that way women were lucky. A purse could hide a multitude of sins or a multitude of guns; Rosie Shepherd's purse held two—guns—and one of them was his. She wore a loose-fitting blouse that looked voluminous enough to double for a maternity top. The skeletonized Ken Null shoulder holster with the little .38 Special revolver was invisible under it, while the blouse was so long that it came halfway down her blue-jeaned thighs.

Holden stopped the car and let his eyes become accustomed to the darkness. He had cut the headlights when they turned off the highway, using running lights only.

Ahead of them was a high chain-link fence. The gates bisected a tarmac driveway and were locked with several strands of chain and a padlock.

"I keep telling myself this should be some kind of trap; it's got all the earmarks. But somehow—"

Holden turned toward Rosie when she didn't finish, her features becoming gradually more discernible in the darkness. "Got a couple of subguns under that blouse, just in case?"

"If you don't like it, I'll stop wearing it."

"I like it," he told her.

"No, you don't. Or you wouldn't say something like that. And no, I don't."

"What?"

"Submachine guns or rockets launchers or anything."

"I like the blouse."

"I'll give it to you. But you'd have to rip out the shoulder pads; your shoulders are broad enough."

"Sweet of you to offer, but I'll take a pass." He smiled, but his skin was still crawling for coming here. What if Steel had planned all this as a setup? Was a live, talking, well-connected FLNAer too good to be true in the literal sense?

Holden drew the bigger of the two Berettas. The gun was beaded all over with sweat from being carried against his body, was slimy to the touch.

The only FLNA captives the Metro Patriots had taken, questioned, then left for the police to pick up on anonymous telephone tips had been street punks who barely understood half the questions put to them, let alone knew anything of consequence concerning FLNA plans, FLNA leadership, or anything of consequence at all. And in this war prisoners were few.

Holden heard the rattle of the chain link and shoved the gun already in his hand toward the sound.

It was Luther Steel. "Only me."

Holden stayed behind the wheel, his right hand on the key switch and ready to hit the ignition. "Pretty deserted-looking," Holden commented for lack of anything better to say.

"We want that look. I didn't know this place existed until six hours ago. Mr. Cerillia borrowed it from the Air Force right after the President ordered this operation.

"I called the director when we made the arrest," Steel went on. "That's when Mr. Cerillia told me about this place." And Steel gestured toward the unimpressive-looking flat-roofed concrete structure behind him, the building as prepossessing as an adobe hut and not dissimilar in size. "No one else knows about it aside from three men on my squad, the three of us—I assume Detective Shepherd is with you—the President, and Mr. Cerillia. Food, weapons, communications equipment. All nestled in the beautifully wooded highlands—"

"Do you know what I'm thinking?" Holden interrupted, smiling.

Luther Steel was through the fence now, letting one of the large gates swing open inward behind him. "Yes, I think I do. If this is some kind of deception, you'll shoot me. Did I guess right?"

Holden started to laugh, saying, "You guessed right."

"So I'm not worried. This isn't some kind of deception. Drive through. I'll walk ahead of you, ride with you, whatever you're comfortable with. The technicians nearly have our man ready."

Rosie Shepherd was out of the car in the next instant, her right hand coming out of her purse with the .45, the .45 leveled at Luther Steel's center of mass. "I thought you said only your men and ourselves knew about this place? Besides the President and your boss?"

"And I stand by that. Everyone who enters or leaves this facility aside from us goes in and out blindfolded. We have two government doctors and a nurse in there. None of them is from this area; all of them have passed security checks personally supervised by the director in the hope that their talents would be needed. The janitorial chores —the place is mainly stainless steel and concrete—we have to take care of on our own. Satisfied, Detective Shepherd?"

"If you're lying," Rosie said, her voice as low as if she were delivering a threat in some cheapie Italian movie. And Holden realized that she was with the next words she spoke. "David won't have to kill you if this is a trap. Because I'll have done it already. I'll walk right next to him, David," she called over her shoulder. Then with a toss of her head she was beside Luther Steel, the gun between them. Before Holden could tell her not to, she'd started walking ahead of the car.

The directions for finding the facility—it was buried deep in the mountains—and all of Luther Steel's message had been delivered to the new Patriot encampment by Lem Parrish, along with a quick summary of a conversation between Parrish and Steel in some bar in Metro.

Holden turned the ignition key and left his lights off, following slowly.

As the car passed between the gates just after Rosie and Steel, Luther Steel turned around. "You want to relock the gate or should I?"

"I'll do it," Holden called back. He put the car in park and stepped out. The Beretta 92-F still in his right hand, he closed the gate, then locked the chain.

He wondered how two doctors, a nurse, the FLNA prisoner, four FBI agents, and Rosie Shepherd and himself could fit in the building. And where were the automobiles?

As Holden started back for the car, Steel called out,

"Park just in front of that Coke machine. Almost let your bumper touch it."

Holden eyed the Coke machine. "Sure." It was old enough to pull a fortune from some Coca-Cola memorabilia collector. What was it doing here?

Rosie still stuck beside Luther Steel like glue. Steel approached the Coke machine, then fumbled in his pockets as though looking for change. Steel *was* looking for change, Holden realized. The FBI man fed the machine as Holden drove up toward it. Steel waved him closer and closer and stepped aside, Rosie still with him.

Steel began pushing the selection buttons in some sort of order, as if—Holden felt the lurch, and then the ground beneath the car began to move, the Coke machine's base very quickly to the level of the car's hood, then above it, Rosie with both fists on her .45. "What the hell's going on, Steel?"

There was darkness darker than the night as Steel's voice said, "Relax, Detective Shepherd. Just relax." Overhead there was a pneumatic thumping sound and then the slapping of rubber gaskets. Red light of the type used aboard a submarine to save night vision when the sub was about to surface washed over the car and Rosie and Steel beside it. Holden stepped partially out of the car, the floor or ground or whatever it was beneath the car still moving downward.

Holden looked up. A gridwork-supported platform was where the opening had been. Holden looked down on a vast open area, concreted, stretching for a considerable distance in all directions, still some thirty feet below.

Holden shouted to Steel, swallowing to pop his ears and relieve the pressure at the same time. "What is this?"

"I told you it was a secret installation the Air Force used."

"For what?" Rosie stood beside Holden now. Her tongue darted out to lick her lips, a nervous gesture he'd seen before. "Easy," Holden told her.

"There are three platforms. When platform one comes down, platform two slides into place. After we reach the bottom, we activate the controls." And Rosie started to move as Steel moved. Holden stayed her with his hand, while Steel produced a folded sheet of paper, not a gun. "I memorized the combination on that old Coke machine, but the thing downstairs I don't have memorized just yet."

"A Pepsi machine?" Holden suggested.

Steel smiled. "That would have been a cute touch, but no. Just an ordinary panel with controls that look something like the controls on a VCR. When you back off the elevator, I'll set them. Then this platform will move into position, and the third platform will rise out of the base just below us. That way there's always a way in and a way out and no waiting."

The elevator stopped. Holden looked around them, seeing the concrete expanse—some sort of huge underground garage—in greater detail. It was not endless, as it had seemed from above, but it did stretch at least 250 yards in all directions. There were various tunnels waiting at its boundaries, and a short distance from the platform were several vehicles that looked like golf carts. They probably were, Holden surmised. But if the government had paid for them, they probably cost ten or fifteen times as much. "What did the Air Force use this place for?" Holden asked, gesturing toward the vast expanse surrounding them.

Steel shrugged. "I don't know. I assume that's on a need-to-know basis, and I don't need to know. But then neither do you. Just guessing, I'd say that for one thing, since they have two elevator setups like this, they stored some sort of strategic heavy equipment down here. There are oil stains on the concrete all around us." Steel stepped off the platform. "I'd guess that at least at one time a considerable number of vehicles were garaged down here."

"There must be guys in the Air Force who still know about this," Rosie said, lowering her Detonics a little— but not much.

"I said that same thing to Mr. Cerillia," Steel told them, walking toward what Holden assumed was the control panel for the elevator platforms.

"Did they use the old Egyptian method?" Holden suggested.

"Have the priests murder the construction crew, then cut out the tongues of the priests? No. Anyway, this isn't a pyramid," Steel said over his shoulder. "Better move that car. Park it anywhere."

As Holden turned to reenter the car, he said to Rosie Shepherd, "Regardless of its shape, let's hope it doesn't turn out to be a tomb, hmm? Stick with Luther."

Rosie nodded as Holden backed the car off the platform. There was a classic screeching sound as Holden maneuvered the vehicle away, then braked. Almost immediately the platform, replete with clay and dust and scrub grass and weeds—was it all plastic?—began to rise, and a third platform rose from beneath it. More imitation plant life.

Holden stepped out of the car. With the 92-F 9mm back under his shirt, he started walking toward Rosie and Steel. "My curiosity is piqued. What if someone just went over the fence and put his money in the machine and pushed the button for his favorite Coke product? Would he get it?"

"An OUT OF ORDER sign flashes, and if he pushes the coin return, he gets his money back. That was covered in the information packet Mr. Cerillia had couriered to me."

"Marvelous," Holden said, nodding.

They started toward the nearest of the golf carts, and Steel gestured for Holden and Rosie Shepherd to ride in back while he sat at the controls. The cart started easily, as properly charged electric vehicles usually did, and Steel chauffeured them smoothly across the open parking area and toward the tunnels at the north of the complex. As Steel drove, Holden took back his second Beretta from Rosie Shepherd's bag, putting the 92-F Compact in his front side pocket. The butt of the pistol stuck out, and the entire shape of the gun was profiled; but he wasn't trying to hide the fact that he was armed.

The electric cart entered one of the tunnels, the rubber tires humming as though the vehicle were passing over a metal bridge. The tunnel was no more than two hundred feet long. At its end there was a tight turn, which Steel navigated slowly. He pulled the cart to a stop beside gleaming stainless-steel double doors on the far side of a corridor considerably narrower than the tunnel and slightly arced, going on in both directions until the line of the exterior arc seemed to meet the line of the interior arc. Perhaps, Holden speculated, the central parking area was analogous to the hub of a wheel, the tunnels being the spokes and the corridor in which they were now being the outer rim.

Holden jumped down and turned around to help Rosie Shepherd, although if he'd ever met a woman in his life who didn't need help, it was Rosie. Single-handedly she had rescued the captured Patriots from Kaminsky and Metro SWAT. All he himself had done, Holden reflected, smiling at her as he assisted her from the vehicle, was get there in time to provide transportation.

"In here," Steel said tersely. He pushed a button beside the doors. They began to part, disappearing into recesses within the walls.

If there was some sort of duplicity, beyond those doors was where its nature would reveal itself. Gentlemanliness being damned, Holden shoved Rosie gently back and followed Steel himself. What lay beyond the doors most reminded David Holden of a television studio, but of vastly greater proportions.

The automatic doors thwacked shut behind them, and Holden almost reached for his guns.

The ceiling was some thirty feet or better above them. Various cables and blackened Erector set-like metal appendages were everywhere. But the floor of the room was divided without actual walls or any sort of partition into several distinct sections. One was very much like a living room of TV studio set quality, the comfortable-looking sofa flanked by two equally comfortable-looking chairs, with a low coffee table equally accessible to anyone on the sofa or chairs at the center. A few yards from this set there was a stainless-steel medical examination table. Over the table there was an oval-shaped structure from which was suspended a white curtain, drawn back and bound. Still another set, this one with desks and office furniture and filing cabinets, was beyond the medical set. There were cots in one corner, a kitchen in another, and a control booth set into the far wall, lit with a rack of long arms on the booth's far wall, their specific nature not discernible at the distance.

"United Artists?" Holden posited.

Steel said, "United States. Follow me, please." Holden

started toward the control booth, cutting through the living room set, taking metal kickplateless stairs upward.

Holden revised his earlier assessment. The facility must have been set up as some sort of very elaborate bomb shelter. It was always a thrilling experience to see how tax money got spent, and the price tag for this place, even if it was twenty years old, had to have been staggering.

At the top of the stairs the door into the control booth was already open. Three persons, two men and a woman, were inside. The doctors and the nurse? Holden wondered. But why should he assume the woman was the nurse? He smiled at his own unconscious chauvinism.

"No real names except my own and those of my men," Steel said as an aside when they entered the control booth. The three persons at the control consoles turned around. Steel went on. "We're using randomly selected names out of a telephone book for the sake of convenience." And Steel gestured to Holden and Rosie Shepherd. "Larry, Sarah, this lovely lady is Eleanor, and she's one of the two doctors I mentioned." Holden stifled a laugh at himself. "This is Tom, and this is Terry," Steel said, introducing the two men. "They run the equipment."

Holden shook the offered hands of the two men and then offered his hand to Eleanor. "Larry," she said, smiling. She was pretty, brown-haired, and blue-eyed, and in about her mid-thirties. Rosie did the handshake round as well. Then Eleanor began to speak. "My colleague Dr. Bob"—suddenly Holden had a flood of memories of his little daughter when they had watched the famous Jim Henson creations and the whole veterinarian sketch, and he turned away and stared through the great sheets of Plexiglas toward the sets below them as she continued—

"will conduct the interrogation with the assistance of Nurse Nancy." Rosie Shepherd unsuccessfully choked back a laugh.

Holden interrupted. "How did G-man Luther here ever get hold of our interrogation subject to begin with?" And he looked Steel straight in the eye.

Steel answered without a blink. "At the second murder scene there was a dog. The dog had a scrap of cloth in his teeth, and after we left, I tried something on a hunch. I couldn't examine the cloth or the dog without disturbing the crime scene, but I wondered if just maybe the dog, in trying to defend the family, had gotten more than cloth for his trouble when he bit one of the attackers. And most emergency medical kits don't contain rabies vaccine. So I started checking. A man had shown up at a clinic in the western suburbs complaining of a dog bite and was still there when we got the lead. We got there before he left and, with the cooperation of the attending physician, put him to sleep. He woke up here. We have a name. Whether it's real or not is unverifiable, but we'll have fingerprint analysis shortly."

The older FBI agent Holden and Rosie Shepherd had met at the previous meeting entered from the opposite end of the control booth and interrupted. "We've got a real name. The name and the prints match up. He is Abdul Wazil. The teletype is still transmitting his rap sheet, and it started about five minutes ago."

"I'd like to see that," Holden interjected.

Luther Steel nodded to Clark.

Dr. Eleanor resumed speaking. "At any event, Dr. Bob and Nurse Nancy will administer certain drugs to this Mr. Wazil. Dr. Bob, who has a varied background in psychotherapy as well as medicine and is quite experienced with interrogation techniques, will ask Mr. Wazil questions. Mr. Wazil's answers, reactions, physical condition, and the like will be monitored on this bank of equipment and through our computer. I'll be up here to analyze and interpret."

Again Holden changed his earlier assessment of just what this place was. Had it been specifically designed for prisoner detention and interrogation? The physical setup below on the studio floor couldn't have been just serendipity; it had to have had some purpose. Was this it?

Rosie volunteered, "Of course, none of this is legal. I mean, you can't use drugs to interrogate a suspect."

Dr. Eleanor said nothing, only looked up toward Steel.

Steel cleared his throat. "These are extraordinary times. I probably like it less than any of you. But we need information more than we need a conviction. He'll be given immunity from prosecution and deported. And I know we have feelings in this room ranging from genuine concern for the rights of the accused to let's-kill-him-when-we're-through-with-him. The latter isn't going to happen."

"Is it all right to smoke around this equipment?" Holden asked. And when no one instantly said it wasn't, he looked at Rosie, who began fishing in her purse. Somewhere along their march up the stairs, Holden noticed suddenly, Rosie had made the Detonics Servicemaster .45 disappear. She gave him a cigarette, started to light it for him, but he took the lighter from her and lit it himself. "So? When do we start?"

Steel nodded to the woman, and she spoke into a microphone, her voice echoing back at them from the studio set up below until Steel closed the door. "Bring in the subject, Nancy."

Nancy was a quite tall blonde somewhere in her twenties, or at least she appeared that age from the distance at which Holden observed. She wore the classic nurse's uniform, wing-shaped white cap and all. She pushed a wheelchair. In it was a man with his head slumped partially forward over his chest. Bob entered from stage right, also classically attired in a white knee-length lab coat, with a stethoscope draped from his neck. Bob and Nancy helped Abdul Wazil out of the wheelchair. After Nancy had fiddled with some sort of control panel built into the stainless-steel table, the table inclined to a gentle diagonal, and together Bob and Nancy leaned Abdul Wazil against the table, secured some restraints, then reinclined the table into a horizontal position. More control fiddling, and the table moved to the level of Bob's waist, which wasn't that high because Bob wasn't that tall. Nancy might wind up with a stiff back by the time the interrogation was concluded because she was considerably taller than Bob.

Television monitors were activated both on the control console and over it as the houselights dimmed. The control room lights dimmed as well. Steel offered Rosie a chair, and she accepted. Holden took a front-row seat beside her—right at the console, Steel joining them. Audio levels were adjusted.

There was a tight shot of a hypodermic syringe in Bob's hand and another tight shot of Nancy placing an IV in Wazil's left forearm. Then she affixed a tube to the IV, and Bob began speaking in English to Wazil.

For some reason Holden had assumed he would somehow understand the interrogation, but on another level of consciousness he had also assumed that Wazil would be spoken to in whatever his native tongue was, likely some form of Arabic or Farsi.

"Just relax, Abdul. You are about to have the most

pleasant sleep you've ever had since you were a tiny baby."

*Abdul Wazil would be the only one,* Holden thought bitterly.

Rosie squeezed Holden's right forearm; her fingers drifted down over his wrist to his hand and stayed there.

"Are you comfortable, Abdul?"

Abdul spoke. "Yes, very."

"That's good. Just rest awhile now. Think the most pleasant thoughts you can; think about the happiest time in your childhood. If an unpleasant thought starts to creep into your mind, I want you to push it aside and go back to that pleasant thought. Just keep reliving it. What are you thinking, Abdul?"

"About my mother."

"Was your mother pretty?"

"She was beautiful, my mother."

"Good. What is she doing, Abdul?"

"She is telling me a story."

"Is it a favorite story?"

"Yes."

"Would you tell me a story? So I can understand just how happy you are, Abdul?"

"Yes."

"Thank you. Tell me all about why you left your home in the Middle East and came to the United States. And start from the beginning because with a story that's just the best place to start."

Holden's fingers were burning from the cigarette, and as he stubbed it out in an ashtray on the console, he became aware of the droning whispering of Eleanor near him. She was giving camera directions.

There was a tight shot of Abdul Wazil's eyes. The pupils were visibly changing shape.

Holden had assumed the eyes would be closed.

Abdul Wazil spoke again. "The Russian told me that coming to the United States would be a good thing. I trust the Russian. So I came. In Europe it was very difficult. The police searched for me, and there was no place where I could be completely safe. I was very tired of changing places to live all the time. I was afraid of the police finding me. I have too much that I must do. The police cannot stop me. And the foreign intelligence agencies. The Russian said it was a good thing, and he made sense."

"Does the Russian have a name, Abdul?"

"Dimitri Borsoi is his name."

"Damn!" Luther Steel gasped.

"Can you ask that creep if this Russian guy uses an alias?" Rosie Shepherd said suddenly.

Eleanor spoke into a microphone a few inches from her lips. "Bob, this is Eleanor. Ask the subject if the Russian he refers to ever uses another name."

Bob nodded almost imperceptibly. "The Russian is your friend, then?" Bob asked.

"Yes," Wazil answered.

"Is he ever called by another name? I might know him, too."

"Mr. Johnson."

# CHAPTER
# 26

Abdul Wazil had the rare knack for spellbinding his listeners.

After the long silence which ensued following Wazil's statement that a Russian named Dimitri Borsoi had been responsible for bringing him to the United States and that the Russian used the alias Johnson, Holden noted various reactions.

Rosie Shepherd exclaimed, "That guy from the truck stop! The one who was trying to get next to the Leopards! Damn, that's Johnson—"

Luther Steel said, "Russian—"

The woman doctor, Eleanor, sucked in her breath.

Wazil resumed speaking, as if he had paused for the dramatic effect he desired, and now that the effect had reached its crescendo, he could continue. "Dimitri said we would win easily. In some ways he was right."

Bob asked, "Why in only some ways, Abdul?"

"The more open the nation, the more easily it is defeated. Freedom of movement. Freedom from searches with warrants. This makes America weak and very vulnerable. But there were other things. Like this election.

Our candidate will win because we are clever. But there are other things."

"What?" Bob asked.

"The United States cannot fight us because the United States is such a place."

"Such a place?"

"Such a place that is open, and there are what the Americans call their special freedoms, and this makes it easy."

"Easy for what, Abdul?" Bob asked.

"Terrorism."

"Are you terrorists?"

"No," Abdul said flatly.

"Are you freedom fighters?" Bob rephrased his question.

"Some of us. Some of us are not."

"Which election?" Bob asked.

"Way to go!" Rosie said enthusiastically beside Holden.

Abdul said, "Metro mayor. A mayor is a very important thing."

"Which candidate are you and Dimitri supporting?"

Rose laughed. "It's a cinch he's not for Costigan." Costigan was the law-and-order, get-tough-on-the-FLNA candidate. Holden agreed that Bob was wasting a question.

"I do not know, and it does not matter. That the election itself must fail is what matters. To help to crush the system here is all that matters."

"Whom does Dimitri Borsoi work for?" Bob asked, dominating the set now.

Around the control booth there were various remarks: "Way to go! . . . Now, yeah! . . . I wanna hear this!"

Three of Luther Steel's FBI agents, including the older guy, had entered the booth a moment earlier.

Holden slapped his hand against the countertop and hissed, "Damn time you asked that, man!"

Abdul said, "He works for—"

Nancy's right hand, a hypodermic in it, moved from behind the skirt of her nurse's uniform, and she stabbed the hypodermic downward into Abdul Wazil's chest, just over the heart.

Both Rosie's and Holden's chairs fell over as they jumped to their feet. Bob reached for Nancy, Nancy wheeled toward him, and the heel of her left hand impacted with the base of his nose. The camera caught the instant hardness of death in Bob's eyes.

Rosie was the first one out the control booth door.

The nurse was running for the double doors through which Holden and Rosie Shepherd had originally entered.

Holden made it out of the control room right on Luther Steel's heels.

Rosie's Detonics .45 was up. Luther Steel had a Sig in both fists and was shouting, "Don't kill her!"

David Holden flipped the railing, came down in an awkward tuck roll on the hard floor, but luckily did not break an ankle. He half fell forward as he threw himself into a run. The blond nurse reached the double doors. Holden heard Rosie Shepherd shout, "Freeze, bitch!"

The doors were starting to open. "Can't they stop the doors in the control room?" Holden shouted as he ran.

Evidently they could not, or no one had thought of it in time.

As the doors opened just enough for the nurse to push through, Holden was right behind her. He dived toward her as she spun toward him, her right leg came up, and he heard the sound of something ripping—her dress, he guessed—as her foot impacted with a glancing blow across Holden's right ear. He was already going for a tackle, and as he dodged left to minimize the effect of her kick, his right hand reached out and groped for something to hold on to. He caught a handful of the front of the nurse's uniform and dragged her down.

Holden hit the floor hard, winded, with his right fist full of torn white fabric. The woman rolled over him and slid across the floor.

Holden grabbed for one of the Berettas. Nancy was on her feet.

Rosie Shepherd's voice sounded calm, almost relaxed, as she said, "You just run, slut! See how far you get with a tailful of this."

Nancy stopped. She turned around.

Nancy's eyes filled with something Holden could only describe as a look of revenge, and it shouldn't have been there. Nancy opened her mouth wide. "Dammit!" Holden threw himself across the few feet separating him from the woman, his right fist bunched, and hammering outward, as hard as he could, he punched her jaw, snapping her head back and sending teeth flying from split lips as the woman tumbled back, hit the floor, bounced, and then lay still.

Luther Steel spoke. "That wasn't necessary, man!"

Holden started to speak.

Rosie Shepherd beat him to it. "This doesn't look like some kinda vitamin pill."

With the point of the Mini-Tanto—maybe it had been under her blouse; Holden didn't know—Rosie Shepherd pushed a small off-white capsule away from two bloody pieces of tooth.

Holden knelt beside the woman, not looking at Luther

Steel or Rosie Shepherd as he spoke. "One time we captured a guy during a mission back in SEAL team days. This guy opened his mouth just like she did. Looked just like she did. That kind of fuck-you look at a time when it was all lost and over and that kind of look shouldn't have been there at all. He bit down hard, and another one of the team said just before the guy got his mouth closed all the way, 'Cyanide.' Your security isn't so terrific, Luther."

David Holden checked the lady assassin's pulse at the throat. She was alive. He tugged at her hair and pulled away the blond wig, revealing shorter hair, a darker shade of blond, beneath it. He took off his windbreaker and draped it over the upper portion of her body. He'd ripped away the right side of her nurse's uniform and most of her bra.

Her breasts appeared to be the only real thing about her.

# CHAPTER

# 27

They sat in the living room set, Holden at one end of the couch, Rosie beside him, Luther Steel in the overstuffed chair farthest away. The older FBI guy, Clark Pietrowski, occupied the near chair. The woman with the phony name of Eleanor sat at the far end of the couch. Steel's other two FBI agents were guarding Nancy in some portion of the underground complex while they waited for her to regain consciousness. The two booth technicians were off at the far end of the soundstage, eating and smoking. Occasionally there was a little laughter from that portion of the huge room which was almost instantly suppressed.

At David Holden's insistence they were doing away with the phony names since there obviously was no security now.

"All right. I'm Rita Harrington. And I really am a doctor. And I thought you were David Holden when you came in with Special Agent Steel. I mean, I read about you in all the newsmagazines—renegade-college-professor-turned-bandit-under-the-guise-of-patriotism and that sort of thing. Anyway, what the hell is going on?"

Steel, his tented fingers parting and moving to his temples, then massaging his temples as though he were suffering from a headache, said, "This was as secure an operation as we could make it. How the hell that woman got in here to kill Wazil—"

"It's *when* she killed Wazil that's most interesting," Holden said.

"I can't see why she didn't do it earlier," Pietrowski almost snarled, lighting a cigarette, exhaling a cloud of smoke. "I mean, she let Wazil tell us Johnson was really Borsoi and that Borsoi was a Russian."

"If she'd made her move too soon," Rosie Shepherd volunteered, "she might have gotten herself nailed before she could finish the job."

"Who is she?" Eleanor—Dr. Harrington—asked.

"She's probably a professional assassin," Luther Steel said wearily. "And she was probably briefed pretty well, which is why she made her move when Wazil was going to say who's behind the FLNA and why she didn't try anything when Wazil was asked which Metro mayoral candidate the FLNA wanted to get elected."

"That was too obvious anyway," Rosie said. "Why would the FLNA support Costigan when he's—" And she shut up, looked up at David Holden, and closed her eyes.

"Costigan," Holden repeated softly.

"She knew Wazil didn't know," Pietrowski said. "Or maybe it didn't matter what he said."

"But Wazil said they wanted to disrupt the election," Steel said, as if thinking out loud.

"And if Roger Costigan's the law-and-order candidate," Holden said, "and Harris Ganby is the moderate, the only candidate who could profit from violence before the election and during the election—"

"The only one who could profit from those mass murders—" Steel interrupted.

"It'd be Roger Costigan," Rosie Shepherd almost whispered. "If the world's going to hell, who do you vote for? The man who hasn't taken a stand on hell or the man who's outspoken about preventing it?"

"Whatever Wazil had said wouldn't have mattered. It's only logical that the FLNA is the enemy of Costigan, and if it wanted any candidate over the other, it'd want Harris Ganby," Steel said, suddenly standing up.

Holden stared at a spot on the coffee table, talking to nobody, to everybody. "If Borsoi is the FLNA leader in Metro and this fake nurse was substituted for the real nurse or however they did it, then her orders came from somebody who can lead us back to Borsoi. If the FLNA all but shuts down the mayoral election over the next few weeks, Costigan's a shoo-in and Costigan's the FLNA's man."

"If that woman got in here," Steel said, while Holden looked up, watching the FBI agent's face and eyes, "then we've got a leak so big—"

"And it can't be with us," Pietrowski said with an air of definitiveness. Then that tone in his voice all but evaporated. "Can it?"

Holden didn't let Steel answer. "No. Somebody between Cerillia and you guys. There have to be aides; there have to be people providing transport, screening personnel records—who the hell got the phony names out of the telephone book? The FLNA's penetrated the FBI."

"Dammit, man," Steel snapped, pushing the overstuffed chair over the edge of the small elevated platform on which the living room set was erected. "Dammit! You're right!"

Holden looked away from Steel and looked at Dr. Harrington. "Rita? Can you wake up Nancy and give her something? Can you do what—what was Bob's real name?

"I never knew. There must be some things with Bob's equipment. But that's not my end of it. We've worked together before, but I was always the controller. He knew his stuff. He was the best at this. At least the best we had. If I administered something, the woman might die."

"Would she talk first?" Rosie Shepherd asked flatly.

Rita Harrington just stared back. . . .

Nancy lay on the steel table, the same one Wazil had been strapped to when she had embolized him with the hypodermic syringe.

Dr. Rita Harrington opened the little cock on the IV tube, and the contents of the plastic sack began to dribble through.

David Holden felt the pressure of Rosie Shepherd's hand in his.

Clark Pietrowski lit a cigarette.

Rita Harrington was using a small remote headset to keep in contact with the two men in the control booth who were monitoring vital signs, working with the computer.

One of Steel's men, the American Indian, cracked his knuckles. Steel said, "That's a great way to build calcium deposits, shit."

Nancy's eyelids began to flutter.

The voice of the one of the booth men was barely audible through Rita Harrington's headset, saying that Nancy was fully under, and the computer was showing that her pulse rate was getting dangerously high.

"Ask her," Holden said simply.

Rita Harrington cleared her throat. "Did Borsoi send you?"

"No."

"Who sent you?"

"Won't—"

"Who sent you?"

"No."

Holden said, "Turn up the amount of IV solution she's getting."

Rita Harrington said, "Her pulse rate and respiration—"

Steel said, "That table has built-in sensing equipment that monitors all the vital data on a computer; it's like having a team of physicians—"

"Is she dying?" Holden asked Rita Harrington.

"She could be."

"Try it anyway," David Holden told her. He felt Rosie holding his hand more tightly.

Steel whispered, "Go ahead. I'll take the responsibility."

"That could be murder," Rita Harrington whispered.

David Holden reached across and turned the cock on the IV tube himself. Rita Harrington grabbed for his hand, and Holden shoved her gently away. "Her—her—it's her pulse rate," Rita Harrington stammered.

Holden asked the question. "Who ordered you to come here if it wasn't Borsoi?"

"Kjel—Kjel—"

Steel growled "It can't—"

"Kjel-strom. Kjel—" Her eyelids sprang open. Her chest rose once and fell.

"She's—she's—" Rita Harrington stuttered.

"Dead." Rosie Shepherd supplied the end of the thought.

"Kjelstrom," Clark Pietrowski said quietly.

Steel seemed to breathe the name. "Tim Kjelstrom."

David Holden just looked at Steel.

# CHAPTER
# 28

"**C**hances are very good that the FLNA knows about the meeting between Mr. Cerillia and Dr. Holden," Luther Steel said. Holden, Rosie Shepherd, Steel's three men—Pietrowski, Runningdeer, and LeFleur—and Steel were in the control booth. The booth was soundproofed, and every wire in the room had been disconnected, every outlet checked. That was no guarantee their conversation was not being monitored, but at least they felt satisfied that they were trying. "Tim Kjelstrom is Mr. Cerillia's administrative assistant. What he doesn't know he could find out extremely easily. If Kjelstrom sent in this female assassin, substituting her for the real nurse, that means he has had complete knowledge of Mr. Cerillia's plans for some time. But on the plus side, Kjelstrom evidently doesn't know the location of this site, or he wouldn't have gambled on just one assassin who could have missed her target. And that is apparently the case, since I doubt he would have resisted the chance to get Dr. Holden. Borsoi might work for Kjelstrom; more likely it's the other way around. In either case, Kjelstrom should know how to find Borsoi. So, if we can get to Kjelstrom—"

"Can't we call Mr. Cerillia?" asked Tom LeFleur, the tall, lean, athletic-looking, sandy-haired agent, his voice sounding devoid of hope.

Through a cloud of cigarette smoke Clark Pietrowski answered. "If Kjelstrom's one of the chief bad guys, we can't contact Mr. Cerillia without a good chance Kjelstrom'd know about it, then rabbit out on us or, worse, kill the director. The only reason we didn't have company at that meeting at the motel was that Kjelstrom probably didn't know what the meeting was about. But by now you should figure word of the meeting is probably all over the FLNA. It's a cinch this Commie guy Borsoi knows the FBI's playin' footsie with the Patriots."

"Couldn't this Johnson or Borsoi or whatever his name is have been coming from a meeting near Metro with Kjelstrom when I bumped into him and that kid from the Leopards at the truck stop?" Rosie Shepherd suggested.

"Distinct possibility." Steel nodded.

"Where's this Kjelstrom guy now?" Rosie asked.

Holden smoked another bummed cigarette, just listening.

"Tim Kjelstrom's usually with Mr. Cerillia. That's probably where he is now," Steel answered.

"Where's the director now, then?" Runningdeer asked.

Steel consulted his wristwatch. "He was in Santa Fe, New Mexico, before the meeting. He was supposed to be in Albuquerque this afternoon for a security conference. Some kind of luncheon. He got so sick from the plane ride, he couldn't make it back by plane without taking something for motion sickness, and the drugs they use make him kind of out of it. So they held the luncheon without him and changed the time of the conference. He took the medication for his motion sickness and flew back. When I notified him concerning Wazil's arrest, he was a hundred percent better."

Holden broke his silence. "What's in Albuquerque?"

Steel looked at him, then looked past him. "There's been a lot of violence in San Diego, El Paso, Laredo, some of the other border towns. FLNA. Some of the violence has been spilling over into Mexico, and relations between the United States and Mexico are severely strained. The recommendation for the joint conference—"

"Lemme guess." Pietrowski laughed. "Tim himself?"

"Who's in charge of security for the conference?" LeFleur asked.

Clark Pietrowski only laughed.

David Holden spoke. "We have several elements to contend with. And they're all of a relatively immediate nature." Holden glanced at his Rolex. It was already well into the next day. "What time does the conference in Albuquerque begin?"

"Ten A.M."

"That's just a little over eight hours from now. So. Borsoi/Johnson knows about our alliance against the FLNA. He won't spread that around. He'll save that. Because if he is supporting Roger Costigan for mayor of Metro, then chances are that a significant number of the local and state elections coming up are set up the same way. He'll save the information about the President and the FBI director acting in concert with the Patriots until the presidential election."

"They'd run their own man for the White House?" Le Fleur said, sounding stunned.

"Not only run but win," Holden told him. "This would be the scandal to end all presidential scandals— acting in defiance of Congress, all that. So Borsoi/Johnson's knowledge about us will keep for a while. We've got to prevent a total disruption of the election in Metro and do what we can in other areas. And we're talking very little time. Weeks. That's it. More events like those mass murders of families of night shift workers, and there'll be more than a drastic economic slowdown. What little law there is will fall apart. The Costigans will sweep into office, and the Front for the Liberation of North America will control whole cities and states officially. Under the guise of cracking down on the FLNA, they'll create such a climate of repression that no one will be able to lift a finger against them. All the FLNA talk about freeing the people of the United States from a repressive government is going to start sounding true. Instead of the American people helping the cops and the Patriots—" Holden couldn't bring himself to say the obvious conclusion.

Rosie, her voice sounding strained, asked, "What about Albuquerque?"

Holden took another one of her cigarettes. "If the FLNA can make things go sour between the United States and Mexico, two things will happen. It'll be easier to foment civil unrest in Mexico—God knows, there's civil unrest in Mexico already—and if the United States has to divert troops to the Mexican border, that's a reduced force to fight the FLNA. We have to carefully evaluate the FLNA's previous attempt on Mr. Cerillia's life. The FLNA was trying to set up the Patriots as the fall guys. If Borsoi/Johnson, or whoever his boss is, is really all that clever, the logical thing would be to hit this security conference in such a manner that the Patriots are blamed for it. That way he not only deepens the impact of Mexican officials getting killed on U.S. soil, because supposedly patriotic Americans are responsible, but he also brands the Patriots as being just as evil as the press and Congress and everybody has been saying. The Patriots would be pretty much out of business as far as getting any help from local police or the citizenry. When he did break the news that Cerillia and the President were in league with the Patriots, he'd be essentially framing the President for being responsible for killing everybody at the conference. If Borsoi/Johnson is that clever."

"I think he's that clever," Luther Steel remarked. He took a riot shotgun down from the rack on the rear wall of the control booth, opened the action, inspected it, and put it back. There were two riot shotguns, Remington 870s, and two M-16s in the rack. There were two Smith & Wesson Model 15 .38 Special revolvers on a shelf beneath the rack, along with boxes of shotgun shells and boxes of 5.56mm ball ammo for the M-16s.

"We're in deep shit," Clark Pietrowski observed.

"Holden, are you thinking what I think you are?" Steel asked suddenly.

David Holden looked at Steel and smiled. "I'll bet I am. I was in Albuquerque once. It was hot, but somehow you could always find a cool breeze coming down off those mountain passes."

"Nobody has to do this," Luther Steel announced, his tone solemn. "I know the location of the conference. The personnel guarding the conference site won't know us from Adam's house cats. They'll be just as likely to kill us as the FLNA people sent against the conference. And even if we make it in, there's not much chance we'll make it out alive again. Clark, Bill, Tom, I can't order you to go."

Bill Runningdeer stood up. "You going, Luther?"

"I've got to go."

"I've gotta go, too," Runningdeer said.

Clark Pietrowski lit another cigarette. "Hell, I'm an

old man. If I'm gonna go out and play commando, I'm gonna sit right where I am until it's time to stand up. No sense wasting my energy until I need to."

"Count me in, Luther." Tom LeFleur nodded.

"Rosie, you go back and—" Holden said.

"Hell, no. Not like the last time."

Holden only looked at her, closed his eyes, and nodded.

"So? What do we do? Steal a plane?" Rosie was enthusiastic.

# CHAPTER
# 29

Stealing an aircraft hadn't proved necessary. Lem Parrish, the disc jockey, was contacted by pay telephone about a dozen miles from the underground facility. Holden asked that Parrish alert the Patriot camp that he (Holden) and Rose Shepherd wouldn't be returning for as long as several days, that he alert Patsy Alfredi to assume command of the Metro Patriot cell in their absence and cancel all pending action. A friend of Lem Parrish's aviator from the Vietnam era named Chester Little, who owned a charter aircraft service, was volunteered by Parrish when Holden asked if Parrish could help them find a pilot.

The available aircraft would accommodate a maximum of eight passengers and crew. There was no time to get together any of the Patriots, and to attempt to go through official or even unofficial channels in the FBI might only have tipped their hand to Tim Kjelstrom and the FLNA.

Holden's shoulder holster for the Beretta 92-F Compact and the Crain Defender knife, along with several spare magazines for the Berettas and for Rosie Shepherd's Detonics .45, had been secreted beneath the spare tire in the trunk of their car. Holden had left the Desert Eagle in camp. As for other gear, such as assault rifles, Special Forces-style eight-inch rise boots, ripstop BDUs, etc., there was an abundance to choose from in the supply stores at the underground facility. Again, the very nature of the facility seemed impossible to discern.

Prewashed black and woodland camouflage BDUs were all that were available, though desert cammie was preferable where they were going. Holden and Rose Shepherd settled for their usual black. They also found Bianchi UM-84 military holsters, webbed equipment belts, Southwind Sanctions accessory sheaths to accommodate virtually any size of fighting knife, belt pouches of all sizes and shapes to accommodate everything from lensatic compasses to shotgun shells. There was even underwear and socks, all of it ready to go.

Since there was no such thing as a male GI of Rose Shepherd's stature, fitting her into available BDU pants and jacket proved challenging.

They took what they needed and left the rest. When they inspected the armory, again Holden revised his opinion of the facility.

The armory was a room about one quarter the size of the soundstage with racks running back to back and facing each other across the center of the room. Along the longer east and west walls crates of ammunition were stacked. At the north and south walls, which were narrower, there were bins of spare magazines and other commonly needed accessories, all neatly stencil-labeled.

There was enough to start a war or finish one.

Not only were there M-16s, as he had expected, but there was also a variety of other weapons: 7.62mm Heckler & Koch G-3s, which, despite their weight, were among the finest battle rifles in the world; the 5.56mm variant G-41s, a recent development for .223 caliber NATO standardization; HK-13 light machine guns; FIE/Franchi SPAS-12, LAW-12, and SAS-12 assault shotguns; MP5-SD3 Heckler & Koch 9mm P integral suppressor submachine guns; Beretta 92-F (M-9) military pistols, such as the one Holden himself carried; Sig-Sauer P-226 pistols; Glock 17 pistols; Walther PP pistols in .22 Long Rifle, suppressor-fitted; gas, sound and light, concussion, and fragmentation grenades; LAWS rockets.

"What is this place?" Rosie asked Holden as he examined one of the shotguns.

"Ever since we got here," Holden told her, "I've been running possibilities. I think the composition of the arsenal here finally makes some sense."

"Whoever stocked this place had terrific taste," Rosie observed, checking one of the HK submachine guns. "These are the best that money can buy."

Holden nodded agreement. "Delta Flight. I still don't have any idea what that studio is for with all the different sets and the control booth. But the massive parking area and all this"—Holden gestured toward the racks—"are a staging area for Delta Flight. You notice the diameter of the opening those elevator platforms make?"

Rosie Shepherd smiled. "I was thinking the same thing. Gunships."

"Gunships," Holden agreed.

"Want M-16s?"

Holden put his arms around Rosie Shepherd. "Tell you what." Holden smiled. "Let me tell you what I want." And Holden kissed her hard on the mouth, and held her for a while. When he looked at his watch, there was time for only one more thing. It was only in the movies that the guy and the girl had one last night together.

Each of them took a rifle and a submachine gun and

Rosie Shepherd took one of the Glock pistols, and they went to join Steel and the FBI team waiting for them at the platform elevator leading up to the fake Coke machine.

# CHAPTER
## 30

For some reason Rose Shepherd had never quite understood, men seemed to consider it virtuous to be tight-lipped.

Their pilot, Chester Little, seemed to exemplify this dubious male virtue. As the last of them stepped down from the business jet's fuselage, Little uttered about the tenth or twelfth sentence to pass his lips since the trip had begun hours before and nearly two thousand miles away on a remote runway better than fifty miles northeast of Metro. "I'll wait until I figure nobody's comin' back; then I'll wait some more; I got time to kill."

"Right," was all Luther Steel said in reply before he walked on. Perhaps Steel was emulating Chester Little? Or did it somehow sound more important to say less?

Chester Little had set down in the desert, and according to Luther Steel's announced best guess, they were somewhere between twenty and twenty-five miles from the site of the security conference, the meeting held on a ranch well south of Albuquerque. They had landed so far from the ranch because all agreed the airspace near the ranch would be secured.

Rose Shepherd walked between David and Clark Pietrowski. For the part of the flight during which she hadn't slept, Clark had shown her photographs of his grandchildren. It was odd to see him like this. He was an old cop, albeit a federal one, but to see him in what he joked about as "Rambo's hand-me-downs" somehow seemed as odd as if she were to see him wearing a tuxedo.

He wore a charcoal-gray V-necked sweater, not a military sweater with elbow and shoulder patches, just an old sweater that looked as if it were made of cotton and that had a few patches, certainly, but all in the wrong places. His revolver was in the same holster he carried it in when he was wearing a suit. No BDU pants, but dark blue pants which looked like something a washing machine repairer would wear. No combat boots, but old hunting boots that looked wonderfully comfortable and even more wonderfully dirty.

Luther Steel walked ahead of all of them. Steel looked more suited to his name than he had before. He was about as well built as David was, and the brown of Steel's skin was darker-looking in the black BDUs and with the black baseball cap's bill shading his face from the strong sunlight. Steel's Sig-Sauer P-226 was at his right thigh in one of the flap-covered Safariland SAS-style holsters, black leather. A Bianchi shoulder rig, one of the little upside-down ones, was the only color that didn't fit; the leather and the elastic crossover strap were chocolate brown. At his left hip was a knife she recognized and approved of: one of the Cold Steel Trailmaster Bowies. Cold. Steel. Hardly.

Rose Shepherd glanced behind her; Runningdeer and LeFleur brought up the rear. Runningdeer and LeFleur carried the same sidearms, Sigs like those Luther Steel carried; their fighting knives were not instantly recognizable. She felt silly thinking it, but she wondered why Runningdeer, a full-blooded American Indian, wasn't breaking their trail.

There was no standardization of small arms, each of the party taking what he or she liked or had faith in or experience with. These ran the gamut from Clark Pietrowski's Remington 870, apparently taken from the control booth rack (the only place she had seen the twelve-gauge pumps) to Runningdeer with an Uzi submachine gun, apparently from the trunk of one of the FBI vehicles.

The plan was to steal one of the security vehicles that would be posted along the access roads, affording them not only transportation but a shared radio frequency as well.

In the overflight while looking for a place suitable for landing, they had spotted several such vehicles, not set as roadblocks but merely parked along the roadside. Uncomfortable-appearing men, looking out of place in sports clothes, stood outside their vehicles for relief from the desert heat, unable to run their cars with the air conditioning because of the potential for overheating.

They angled toward the rough compass bearings they had logged during the overflight and walked in silence. When Luther Steel signaled a halt, Rose Shepherd brought her M-16 rifle up from patrolling carry to a ready position.

David moved up beside Steel, and they conferred in whispers she could not fully hear. Clark Pietrowski hissed to her, "Take it easy, Rosie."

"I'm cool, Clark." She nodded back.

David signaled toward the rocks to the west beneath which they had moved for the last twenty minutes; Rose signaled the two men behind her, and she started up a wide, shallow, tumbleweed-choked defile.

The rocks were already too hot to touch.

She watched as David and Luther Steel ran forward. . . .

David Holden dropped to his knees beside Luther Steel, Steel already behind the cluster of upthrusting barrel cacti about a hundred yards from a blue full-size Ford station wagon. Looking overheated, two men, with windbreakers on to cover their guns, paced near the car.

Holden whispered to Steel, "Will they drop their guns if it looks like they don't stand a chance? Or will they fight?"

"They'll fight."

That was the answer David Holden had thought Steel'd give.

Holden surveyed the ground immediately between the cacti and the blue station wagon. It was barren, affording no cover for a hundred-yard sprint. But to the South there was a dry wash leading almost to within spitting distance of the road and about twenty yards or so of the two security men.

Holden leaned close to Luther Steel, whispering almost directly into his ear. "I'll head through the wash. When you figure I'm there, step out and cry out for help. Strip off your weapons and the BDU jacket. Show your badge."

The muscles in Steel's face drew tight; the tendons in his neck distended. "This sucks. Yeah, go ahead."

Holden glanced toward the road again, then was up, moving. The G-3 was strapped across his back, and he held one of the silenced Heckler & Koch submachine guns in his right fist.

He reached the wash and slid down into it, the palm of his left hand abrading on a rock. He was up quickly, sprinted along the length of the wash in a low crouch, and was almost to the road when he heard Luther Steel's voice.

"FBI—I need help!"

As Holden hit the near point to the road and clambered up out of the wash, both the security men turned toward Steel, backs toward Holden as he hit the pavement. Their guns looked drawn, as seemed only logical.

Holden moved at what appeared to him like a snail's pace, narrowing the gap between himself and the two security men. Twenty yards. Fifteen. Luther Steel was saying he needed their help to combat a plot against Rudolph Cerillia. Steel seemed almost terminally honest, a good and increasingly rare quality, Holden reflected.

Ten yards.

Seven. "Nobody moves!" And Holden fired a burst from the submachine gun into the road surface between the two men. "You're covered on all sides! Twitch and this subgun cuts you both in half!"

The two men froze, hands slightly away from their sides, their guns visible.

Holden narrowed the gap to fewer than three feet. "Play it cool and nobody gets hurt," Holden advised them as with his left hand he relieved one man of a Smith & Wesson Model 13 .357 Magnum three-incher, the other of a gleaming stainless-steel Smith & Wesson Model 645 auto.

Steel disappeared behind a cactus for an instant, then reappeared with an M-16 in one hand and an Uzi in the other, running toward the two men.

David Holden breathed. . . .

* * *

Holden studied the map found in the glove compartment. Why it was there was another question. It showed the ranch house complex in considerable detail, not just roads in and out. One of the two men spoke. "Look, we'll help you if you guys are really who you say."

It was the man from whom he'd taken the S&W .45. Both men, hands cuffed behind them, sat in the meager shade afforded by the station wagon, which was pulled well off the road. In the corner of the map some numbers were scrawled.

"I don't think so," Holden told them, walking closer to the car. Holden showed the corner of the map to Steel and Pietrowski. While the two men looked at the numbers, Holden called out to Rose Shepherd, who was nearest the Ford's front seat. "Rosie, try this frequency on the radio, but write down the setting it's on." He read off the numbers from the map.

Holden had flicked off the radio when they'd moved the car. Only routine security force traffic had been coming over it, a shortwave rather than CB.

In a moment there was static; then after another moment there was a voice. The voice was reading numbers.

"What do those numbers mean?" Steel demanded, crouching in front of the two prisoners.

The second security man spoke. "I don't know what the hell—"

Clark Pietrowski raised the Remington 870 and settled the roughly .72-caliber muzzle over the tip of that man's nose. "Each pellet in this thing is about the size of a .30-caliber rifle bullet, friend. Imagine what will happen to your face in the coupla seconds before you die."

The man's voice sounded odd with his nose pinched. "You—you—"

"Wouldn't do it? Naw. Now, *he* wouldn't do it." And Pietrowski grinned as he nodded toward Luther Steel. "I don't know if anybody else'd do it. But me? I'd do it. And I'm gonna unless you tell us everything you know and make me feel real confident it's all true. Got that?" And Pietrowski racked the pump. The sand between the second man's legs started going dark, and the smell of urine filled the air. Clark Pietrowski looked up, saying, "You know, he's smart; he believes me."

The numbers formed a simple code, detailing procedures as they were taking place. The frequency belonged to the Front for the Liberation of North America. And so did the two security men, the one with the shotgun to his nose quickly admitting that Tim Kjelstrom had personally recruited the right personnel for important road access points.

A fast, shaky-voiced description of the number sets revealed that the assault on the ranch house where the security conference was being held had already begun.

"We're too late," LeFleur said.

Holden and Steel said it almost as if they had rehearsed it. "No, we're not."

On impulse Holden told Rose Shepherd, "Switch back to the other frequency."

After a few seconds the radio chatter changed. Just routine security calls. "They either have their own man running the radio center or they're playing tapes," Bill Runningdeer said thoughtfully.

Rose Shepherd fired the Ford's ignition. "So?"

Holden told LeFleur and Runningdeer, "Move those pieces of shit into the shade so they don't start to smell too fast." And David Holden started around the front of the Ford, calling to Rosie Shepherd, "Move over. I'm driving."

# CHAPTER

# 31

The main gate to the ranch property, according to the map, was some two miles from the house. As they approached the gate, Holden said, "They won't use explosives until the very end. Fire and smoke would be visible from the air and bring in the air cover and the road security the FLNA doesn't own."

"How do we tell the good guys from the bad guys?" Rosie Shepherd asked.

"The ones who are armed and alive will most likely be the bad guys, Detective," Steel intoned.

"He's got a point, kiddo," Clark Pietrowski chimed in. "If Tim Kjelstrom set this up right, half the guys on the inside put the lights out on the other half and the FLNA owns that place by now."

Two cars, both mid-size GM products, were parked to wedge-block the road just in front of the gate.

Four men with M-16s were visible beside the cars.

"They can't be legit," Rosie said.

"We can't risk killing them if they are," Steel reminded them. Steel sat on the far front passenger side; Rosie Shepherd sat between Holden and Steel.

"Runningdeer!" Holden shouted. "Roll over the seat back, and get ready to use that LMG." One of the HK-13 light machine guns had been hauled along by LeFleur and Runningdeer, then set up facing the rear deck. Holden hit the dashboard switch to lower the station wagon's rear window.

"Slow up about here," Steel ordered.

Holden advised Steel, "Don't get yourself killed."

"Be careful, boss," Pietrowski added.

Steel pushed open the front passenger door and reached out. He held the doorframe as he leaned his upper body out of the car. "Federal agents. This is my identification!"

Holden shouted it as Rosie Shepherd screamed it: "Get back!"

All four brought up their M-16s to assault positions— not the most accurate firing position at the distance—and opened up. The Ford's windshield spiderwebbed as Holden swerved and Steel slammed back into the car, Rosie Shepherd dragging him half across her chest. Pietrowski shouted, "Maybe they just don't like black people, Luther!" Holden glanced right again, Rosie clambered over Steel, punched the adopted Glock 17 out the open window as the door slammed, and twisted the muzzle left and right, spraying toward the gate.

Already there was answering fire from the side windows, from Pietrowski and LeFleur. Holden locked the emergency brake as he cut the wheel hard right, shouting, "Hang on!" The Ford bootlegged into the middle of the highway, Holden recovering the wheel as he called out, "Runningdeer, we're backing up! Use the machine gun!"

Holden hauled the selector into reverse as he popped the emergency brake. The smell of burning rubber was strong. Then he stomped the gas pedal. As he looked over the front seat, he could see Rosie and Luther Steel each firing from the front passenger window, Pietrowski and LeFleur firing handguns out the open rear doors, and Runningdeer prone on the back deck, the tailgate folded down, firing the machine gun.

Hot brass buzzed Holden's face like a swarm of angry hornets.

Two of the gate guards were already down. A third hurtled himself over the hood of one of the cars, while the fourth threw his rifle away as he jumped into the other car. The second car started moving. Then the two rear tires blew out, and it dropped like a stone on its rear axle and skidded across the tarmac, sparks flying in its wake.

The third man pushed up, firing an M-16 from one hand, a pistol from the other, but a fusillade of gunfire cut him down. The station wagon's engine was humming so loud Holden thought he would throw a rod.

The fourth man was out of the dead car, running. Pietrowski shouted, "Keep your head down, Bill!" Runningdeer went flat, and the .357 Magnum in Pietrowski's right fist thundered, and the fourth man dropped to the road surface.

"I'm braking—watch it!" Holden slowed, stopped, the front end swerving a little as he worked the wheel. "We're coming around!" Holden gave it gas, cut the wheel, shrugging the rear end into a diagonal, into drive again, and stomped the gas pedal. He punched through the half-shot-away gate and swerved around the mid-size GM car, still parked, then into the oncoming lane to avoid the fourth gate guard's body and the second car that was wrecked.

The engine light was on.

Holden didn't care as he smashed the accelerator pedal to the floor.

"Everybody be ready to clear the vehicle when we stop. She's getting hot!" Steam or smoke was rising from the hood on all sides, and the engine was knocking badly.

About a quarter mile along the road's course, densely planted tall deciduous trees flanked the road on both sides, and the grass—unnatural here—which formed an apron before the trees was as neatly trimmed as if it were manicured.

Holden kept the pedal to the floor and heard the sounds of magazines interchanging, bolts being worked. He picked a piece of hot brass from inside his BDU front.

"Right up to the house—that's the only way," Steel announced.

"Steel, you and LeFleur and Runningdeer take the right. Rosie and Pietrowski and I'll take the left side," Holden ordered.

"Sounds good to me." Steel nodded as Holden looked toward him.

Ahead of them, over the sick sound of the engine, Holden heard gunfire. "Once we know it's safe, let's toss a grenade into the car. The explosion and the fire should draw in the air cover," Holden told them.

There was a Mercedes parked by the side of the road. As they sped past it, Holden caught sight of the driver, eyes staring up into the sun, a hole in the windshield about the size of a grapefruit just level with the head.

The engine was making sounds Holden had never heard a car make before. He could smell something burning. "Remember! Out as soon as we stop. We may not need that grenade."

The ranch house spread before them as they rounded a

bend, the other side of the bend blocked from view along the access road by the trees.

It was hardly a little ranch house.

At the far end of a green-carpeted formal garden stretching for more than the length of a city block and highlighted by shrubbery clipped and sculpted after the fashion of bizarre animal shapes lay a patio/driveway. A massive stone fountain at the driveway's center jetted water high into the air. Just beyond the fountain lay the house itself, rising three stories above the ground level, of Mediterranean influence with a dull red tile roof, exterior stucco, and immaculate. A mansion in the desert.

There was hand-to-hand combat on the steps to the house, but the driveways on each side of the greenway were blocked by vans with armed men using them as cover. As Holden turned the station wagon toward the base of the Y-shaped driveway, he realized the rest of the way would have to be on foot. "I'm going to slow to a crawl, and everybody get out. Then I'm ramming the car into that van on the right, and there's our explosion. Anybody got an M-16 they don't need?" One was shoved toward him.

He felt the pressure of Rosie's hand on his right forearm, but she said nothing.

"Start getting out!" Holden commanded.

The doors opened. In the mirror he saw Runningdeer with the LMG bailing out the back across the tailgate. Pietrowski and LeFleur exited from the rear passenger seat. Steel shouted, "Good luck!" and was gone from the front passenger side.

Rosie's voice came to him calmly. "You can't ram them and shoot at them at the same time. It's no use to tell me not to." He heard the rattle of a sling swivel.

"All right."

Holden began to accelerate.

He turned the wheel into the right arm of the Y and put the accelerator to the floor. The engine barely responded. Flames licked up suddenly where the hood met the fenders, and the windshield was smudged black from burning oil.

Rosie was coughing. And then the sound of her coughing was lost in the sound of gunfire as she opened up on the men near the van. Bullets pinged off the bodywork; more of the windshield shattered. Holden's head was down as low as he could keep it and see. Black smoke began billowing from around the hood in great clouds.

"Get ready!" Holden shouted.

"I was born ready!"

It was Ward Bond's line from a John Wayne western. And suddenly Holden laughed. "Out! Now!"

"I've got your rifle!" Rosie sang out.

Holden jammed the butt of the M-16 to the accelerator pedal, wedging the flash hider at the muzzle end into the upholstery. Rosie was already tumbling out as Holden threw open his door and rolled.

He hit the gravel driveway surface hard and flat, his wind gone for an instant. Gunfire tore into the driveway surface near his head. His eyes squinted against the gravel dust as he pushed himself up and dived over a concrete fence onto the grass. He rolled onto his back as he stabbed the MP5-SD3 toward the van. In the same instant the station wagon struck the van broadside.

Holden rolled onto his face, covering his eyes, his ears ringing with the sound, and the ground beneath him seemed to tremble. He was up, stumbled, ran, flipped the fence. "Rosie!" A black-and-orange fireball belched toward the clear blue desert sky; chunks of shrapnel and burning fabric rained down. Holden shielded his eyes. "Rosie!"

"Here! I'm all right!"

He saw her, skirting the van along the grass and into the gravel driveway, angling toward the center greenway.

Holden ran toward her, sidestepping something that looked like a charred human arm, and when he was within a yard of her, she tossed him the G-3, shouting, "Catch, David!"

He caught.

His thumb spun the safety tumbler, and side by side they broke into a dead run along the grass. At the far left edge of Holden's peripheral vision, he could see Pietrowski waiting for them, laying down suppressive fire toward the steps of the house with his shotgun. Holden glanced to his right. Steel, Runningdeer, and LeFleur were working their way forward, guns blazing, toward the steps.

There was gunfire coming down on Pietrowski from the second van.

Holden wheeled toward the van and fired the G-3 toward two of the gunmen. It put both men down, blew out one of the tires, and shattered one of the west coast mirrors.

The other gunmen retreated behind the van. Holden dumped the empty magazine and rammed a fresh twenty-rounder up the magazine well. Rosie Shepherd shouted, "Watch this, David—star of the softball team!" The grenade arced high and dropped just at the front of the van. Holden sprinted away. Rosie hesitated for a moment, then ran after him. As he glanced back, the grenade went off, rocketing the van's front bumper skyward. The entire vehicle shuddered, then flipped over on its side as a fireball engulfed it, then rose skyward.

Pietrowski was running, firing, feeding the pump shot-gun, constantly firing.

There was a concentration of FLNAers on the steps. Most resistance to them was halted, and bodies littered the area between the fountain and the steps.

Pietrowski reached the fountain, pinned down at last. Holden forced Rosie Shepherd down behind a granite obelisk, while assault-rifle fire from the height of the steps tore chunks out of the obelisk. Holden grabbed for the MP5-SD3, stabbed it around what little protection the obelisk afforded, and fired it one-handed, spraying to right and left. He cleaned the magazine, tucking back under a hail of answering fire.

Rosie was up, flattened against the side of the obelisk, her M-16 spraying full-auto bursts across the height of the steps.

Holden had a fresh magazine in the HK submachine gun. He let it fall to his side on its sling, then drew the full-size Beretta as Rosie tucked down beside him. "Load up. When we get close to the fountain, make another one of those sensational throws, okay?"

"Gotcha." Rosie smiled.

Holden shifted to a twenty-round magazine for the Beretta, the Beretta going to his left hand, the HK in his right. "You ready?"

Rosie had the M-16 in her right hand and a submachine gun identical to Holden's in her left. The Detonics and the Glock were thrust into the web belt that held up her BDU pants. "Ready!"

"Now!" Holden broke from cover, staying along the fence line, Rosie beside and a little behind him as he looked back once.

There was an explosion inside the house, chunks of roof tile blowing everywhere.

Holden opened fire toward the steps, short bursts with the submachine gun in his right hand, double taps with the Beretta in his left.

They were nearly at the fountain. Pietrowski opened fire again, and the FLNA defenders fell back. "Right onto the porch, Rosie!" Holden shouted, firing both weapons from shoulder level as he ran for the fountain. Rosie let both her weapons drop on their slings as she pulled a grenade from her web gear, then hurtled it. He saw the hit as she took it and went down. "No!"

The grenade struck the concrete porch, bounced, exploded in midair. Holden skidded to his knees on the concrete of the driveway beside Rosie.

"I'm all right. God, it hurts!" She was holding her left shoulder, but the submachine gun was back in her left hand as Holden shielded her with his own body while she got to her knees. The submachine gun opened up. Holden fired out his own sub, then emptied the Beretta toward the steps.

Pietrowski stormed the steps, took at least one in his right leg, and went down like a falling rock, rolling down the steps, his shotgun discharging once.

"I'm with you!" Rosie shouted.

Holden stabbed the Beretta into his belt, reached for the G-3, and ran toward the steps.

He heard a short burst from Rosie's submachine gun, then, a half second later, the flat boom of her .45. One of the FLNA defenders ran forward, firing a submachine gun toward Pietrowski. Holden fired the G-3 at the same instant Pietrowski fired his revolver, and the man went down. Holden reached Pietrowski. Pietrowski shouted, "Get up those damn steps now!"

Holden left him, taking the steps three at a time in a dead run. An FLNAer came at him from the left, and

before Holden could fire, he heard the sound of Rosie's
.45, and the man dropped.

At the top of the steps now, FLNAers were everywhere. Holden fired the G-3 from a hard assault position.
He let the empty weapon drop to his side on its sling as
his left hand ripped the second Beretta from the shoulder
holster under his left arm.

An FLNAer with an Uzi rose from behind an overturned concrete urn. Holden fired the Beretta left-
handed, double-tapping the man in the throat and face.
The Uzi slipped from the man's fingers.

Holden skidded to his knees beside the man, ducking
for cover behind the urn as he grabbed the Uzi. Gunfire
sprayed from the pillared central entryway. Holden
stabbed the Uzi over the top of the urn and sprayed it
out. He tucked back as chunks of the urn blew away from
answering fire.

Holden rammed a fresh magazine up the well of the
HK submachine gun, then did the same for the G-3. He
saw Rosie Shepherd and shouted, "Stay back!" She was
just below the height of the steps, flat across them, and
firing the Glock toward the pillared entryway.

Holden started to his feet. Luther Steel vaulted the
railing at the far end of the porch, gesturing to LeFleur to
break off, presumably to aid Pietrowski. Runningdeer
was right behind him.

"The entryway!" Holden shouted, pointing with the
G-3 toward it.

"Right!" Luther Steel skipped over a dead FLNAer
and angled away from the steps. David Holden was up,
running, the big Beretta reloaded with the second twenty-
rounder.

Beyond the pillars lay an interior garden. FLNA personnel were firing down from the second-floor balconies

on each side; a few were on ground level. Holden fired the submachine gun, hearing more gunfire beside him. Chunks of marble and concrete exploded, shrubbery was mowed down, and the FLNAers fell.

Gunfire tore into the marble steps just ahead of him, and Holden dived left, over the end of the steps, and came down in a roll into a hedgerow. The hedges were defoliated as he moved, gunfire from above ripping into the hedgerow and the grass. Holden stabbed the HK submachine gun toward the balcony opposite him and fired it out. One FLNAer tumbled over the railing, screaming as he fell.

At the roar of a shotgun Holden looked right. Pietrowski, in the pillared entryway, fired at the opposite balcony.

Luther Steel shouted, "Cover me!" and sprinted into the open, firing an M-16 from each hand toward the balconies, going for the rose-trellised far wall.

Steel hesitated for an instant, stumbled, then kept running. Holden guessed Steel was hit, but not too badly.

Holden reached the far wall, eyeballed the distance to the balcony above him, tore a grenade from his web gear, counted the seconds, then lobbed it onto the balcony with his left hand. He tucked tight into the corner where the walls met as the explosion came.

When he looked up, he saw Rosie Shepherd, pitching grenades into the other balcony, as fast as she could recover from one, lobbing the next. The explosions came almost in series, one, then another, then another, then another, the entire opposite balcony falling away in massive chunks as FLNAers screamed.

Holden lobbed another grenade onto the balcony near him, then ran to join Luther Steel, shouting to Rosie as he ran, "Stay down!"

There was an arched entryway at the center of the wall between the rose trellises. Luther Steel crouched there, firing an M-16 toward the balcony beneath which Holden had just taken shelter.

But Steel held the rifle awkwardly.

As Holden dropped down beside him, Holden saw why. Steel's left hand was covered with blood. "Nailed my shoulder and upper arm. I'm okay. Somebody's gotta get to that second floor. If Mr. Cerillia and the others are—"

"Yeah," Holden snarled. Bill Runningdeer was doing a broken-field run across the interior garden, with very little gunfire aimed toward him. Maybe that was a good sign. Holden loaded a fresh magazine into the submachine gun, unslung the G-3 and the bag with the G-3's spare magazines. "Here, you might get more action for it than I will." Holden left Steel, a stairway on either side of him leading toward the balconies. He went to the left. Not much remained of the other balcony anyway.

Hugging the side wall, taking the steps three at a time, he met no resistance and reached the second floor. It was all open here, and along the length of the balcony was a series of louvered doors, some of them blown inward, some still closed.

He smelled smoke and remembered the explosion he had heard from inside the house moments earlier.

Shots were still coming from the ground level, Holden's own G-3 from the sound of them. Two men darted out of one of the blown-out doorways and fired over the balcony. Holden stepped out, and a series of short bursts from the submachine gun put them down.

Holden kept close to the wall, stepping over the FLNA dead, reaching down to grab up an Uzi for his left hand, trying to differentiate the smell of smoke from the dust raised by the grenades.

He heard Bill Runningdeer's voice behind him. "I'm with you, Professor Holden!"

Holden called back to him, "They're in here someplace."

At the opposite side of the balcony there was a double doorway, and as the doors opened, Holden almost opened fire. It was Rosie, left arm tied with a bandanna at the bicep and limp at her side, right hand holding the Glock pistol.

Holden gestured toward the door, which he approached now. Rosie Shepherd nodded back.

The smoke smell—maybe plastique; it could have been that—was very strong here.

David Holden stopped beside the doorway and turned half away from it, then mule-kicked his right foot against the door. The door sprang back, then swung open outward. Holden pulled it all the way back. Rosie was on the opposite side. Bill Runningdeer was behind him.

Holden drew the Defender knife. He quickly and carefully cut one of the grenades free of his equipment, leaving the pin in place. He shot Rosie Shepherd a grin, then lobbed the still-pinned grenade through the door opening. Holden threw himself through after it.

Runningdeer's Uzi sprayed across the ceiling to keep anyone in the room from opening fire. Holden flattened himself on the floor behind an overturned wooden desk.

There was no gunfire.

Holden gambled. "Kjelstrom?"

He was almost surprised when a voice answered him. "Get out!"

"What happened here?" He gambled again. "The plastique not work like you figured?"

"Get out!"

"Where's your boss—I mean, Cerillia?"

There was no answer.

Holden heard Steel's voice behind him; the man was tough. "This is Luther Steel, Tim. Look. Whatever happened here, maybe it isn't the end of the world, all right?"

The smell of the plastique was so overpowering, Holden was almost starting to get high from it.

Cerillia's voice. Fast. Pained. "He's got the whole place wired to go—" There was a thudding sound and then a groan.

Holden peered around the edge of the desk. Through an open doorway a long, almost medieval room was visible. A conference table ran down its center, with persons sitting up in chairs or slumped over the table, and a marble-manteled fireplace was at the far end. All the people wore business suits; all were middle-aged or past that. Some had visible wounds. A few had noticeably mortal wounds. At least two had lost parts of their bodies. Some of them might be alive, too, Holden realized.

Taped to the ornate legs of the table and chairs were pinkish-gray ropes of plastique. Down the center of the table was what looked like a massive blackened snake. Holden realized what had happened. Something had gone wrong, some of the plastic explosives had gone off when they shouldn't have, and a lot of the rest had burned.

A gaping hole was visible in the room over the conference chamber.

"Kjelstrom? You all right?" Holden called out.

"Get the fuck outta here. You lost."

"I don't think so." When Cerillia had called out, Kjelstrom hadn't shot Cerillia.

David Holden stood up, leaving the captured Uzi behind the desk.

"David!" It was Rosie's voice, calling to him.

"It's okay," Holden called back. He let the MP5-SD3 fall to his side on its sling as he walked forward.

"Don't come any closer, man! This pig country's gonna feel wrath!"

"You're full of shit," Holden answered calmly. "So shoot me, Timmy." Holden quickened his pace. As he stepped into the conference room, a young man in a tattered three-piece suit was splicing together wires for some sort of battery-powered detonator rigged into the biggest block of plastique Holden had ever seen.

"You lost!" Kjelstrom shouted as he brought the wires together to make the contact and detonate the explosives all around the room.

When David Holden had let loose his submachine gun, he had drawn the Beretta 92-F. It was behind Holden's right thigh, and Holden brought it forward and raised the pistol to eye level as his right first finger drew back on the trigger double action.

Kjelstrom was fewer than ten feet away, and it wasn't much of a shot. The left side of Kjelstrom's face was badly burned, and part of one trouser leg was burned away as well from the accident with the plastique.

"No, you lost." And so had the FLNA this time.

David Holden shot administrative assistant and traitor Tim Kjelstrom twice at the bridge of the nose. Tim Kjelstrom's hands went limp, the wire contacts fell from his fingers, and his body slapped back against the wall and just lay there while the blood began oozing out all over his face.

# CHAPTER

# 32

Cerillia and most of the attendees at the security conference would survive, some of them (like Cerillia himself) barely injured. The shock and the bad dreams might go away eventually. Two of the United States Justice Department people, one official from the Mexican Federal Police, an official with the United States Border Patrol, and a Texas police chief had died.

Seventeen special federal security officers (loyal) were dead; another eight injured, but none of them critically.

Forty-three FLNAers, most of them probable gang members from the various large cities on the U.S. side of the border, some of them apparently foreign nationals, had died. A few were critically injured and not expected to survive.

In the next instant after he shot Kjelstrom, Holden felt Rosie Shepherd standing beside him.

He held her hand.

Then Luther Steel, despite his wounds, took charge. Medical personnel were called up from all over the Southwest and helicoptered in, while a special FBI counterterrorist bomb disposal team was dispatched by jet from Los Angeles.

Rosie Shepherd's wound was pronounced superficial by the physician. Tom LeFleur was hauled away from a lunch counter in the whistle-stop town seventeen miles to the east. By that time the doctors flown out from Albuquerque were already attending to the most seriously injured among the dignitaries and the security personnel. To Luther Steel's credit, and Clark Pietrowski's, both men refused medical treatment until the more seriously wounded were attended to.

After Rosie's arm had been bandaged by the country doctor and she'd been given a tetanus shot and an antibiotic shot, the country doctor was whisked away again under threat of being in violation of national security if he opened his mouth.

Bill Runningdeer found the keys to a Mercedes, and Luther Steel told Holden and Rosie Shepherd, "Get out of here before anybody realizes who you guys are. When I get back to Metro, I think we've got some business to attend to with that election."

As Holden drove, Rosie leaned her head on his right shoulder and slept, and he thought about all that. Business. Election. Borsoi/Johnson.

He turned off the main road when he spotted what he hoped was a familiar combination of rock, juniper, and cactus, keeping the Mercedes nice and slow. He kept it that way for almost a half hour, the ranch road deteriorating rapidly the deeper it penetrated into the desert.

"David?"

"Yes?"

"I just wanted to know you were here."

"Always," David Holden told Rosie Shepherd.

And in the distance he could see Chester Little's charter jet.

"You rest. I'm here." Holden hit the horn button a few times to let Little know they both were here.

**Scott McKenna blasts his way through Burma in *Hell Wind in Burma*, the fourth book in the Shadow Warrior action adventure series, available December.**

An ordinary man would not have heard the very slight sound of a human being disturbing the air. McKenna, his back facing the curtained doorway to the south, did. He spun in time to see a man's raised right arm, the hand extended in a sword-ridge Shuto, coming down at him.

That microsecond made the difference. Catching sight of two other men by the curtained doorway, McKenna reacted with astounding speed. He took a step forward with his left foot, and, as the man's arm came downward, gripped the attacker's right wrist with his left hand, and the man's right hand with his right hand. Kakuzo Seiyukai's own momentum put him at a disadvantage for a moment, giving McKenna time to pull the captured arm up and out, and permitting him to apply the first pressure by bending the fingers back.

The Dragon Claw Ninja, who had tried to sneak up on McKenna and break his neck with one Shuto chop, received his second surprise when McKenna stepped clockwise with his right foot, jerked Seiyukai's right arm over his left shoulder, then applied the second pressure by lowering the ninja's arm over his shoulder—all of it within half the time it takes to blink an eye.

For the takedown McKenna placed his left foot in front of the side of Seiyukai's right foot, and continuing the diagonal pressure and twisting his upper body to assist the action, he pulled. Seiyukai had no choice but to go along with the pressure. In an instant he found himself helpless, on his knees, his face only a foot from the floor. McKenna had used a simple Aikido over-the-shoulder lock to wreck Seiyukai's action.

The most beautiful of all ritualized weaponless fighting, Aikido is neither possible nor practical for street defense. Its techniques are too intricate, take too long to learn (from five to fifteen years for a high level of proficiency), and require constant practice; but *ninjitsu* is a combination of many forms, and McKenna was a master of them all.

It was Murad Tabriz and Kesar Gama, the two Punjabis from India, who saved Kakuzo Seiyukai's life. Before McKenna could kick Seiyukai either in the side or the front of the neck, he had to release him to avoid the attack of the two Punjabis coming at him like two express trains, the wide-faced Tabriz armed with a Malaysian *kris,* Gama with a *badik,* a wide-bladed Indonesian slashing knife.

Giving Seiyukai's right arm a final vicious twist, McKenna released him and moved back to meet an enraged Tabriz, coming at him from the right, while Gama stormed in from the left. The two Indians were not tall. They were brawny, tough, and proficient in Kalaripayit, the South Indian martial art.

Kakuzo Seiyukai—in more agony from severely wounded pride than from the pain in his right arm and shoulder—scooted backward very rapidly toward the curtained door, his face twisting with rage and hatred. He didn't know the identity of the man who had put him down so easily. He did know that whoever he was, he was an expert in Aikido! The fool! Aikido was not a match for *ninjitsu*! It didn't matter. Gama and Tabriz would kill him very quickly.

But the two Punjabis didn't kill McKenna very quickly. Slightly ahead of Gama, Tabriz came in fast, the *kris* in his right hand held low and in position for a fast stomach stab and upward slash.

Keeping an eye on Seiyukai and Gama, McKenna did the unexpected. He made a high leap and executed a Tae Kwon Do Tolyo Chagi roundhouse kick—so fast that Murad Tabriz never saw it coming. He only felt the explosion of crucifying agony as the heel and sole of McKenna's left foot broke off most of his teeth, broke his upper jaw and nasal bones, and fractured his lower jaw. Tabriz dropped the *kris,* staggered back, and, weak from shock and gagging on blood, found himself sinking to the floor.

Taken aback by the sudden turn of events, Kesar Gama decided not to take any chances. From the corner of his eye he saw that Kakuzo Seiyukai had jumped to his feet with the speed and the grace of a jungle cat and was moving toward McKenna.

Gama made his move at the same time that Seiyukai charged and first feigned with a Yoko Geri ball of the foot kick, then turned and attacked with a right Ushiro Geri spinning kick, aimed at McKenna's solar plexus.

Gama switched the *badik* to his left hand and attempted a downward slash across the right side of McKenna's neck, the light reflecting off the wide, shiny blade.

McKenna stepped back slightly and to his left, simultaneously blocking Seiyukai's kick with a right forearm Palmok block, his quick movement saving him from Gama's Makassarese *badik*.

Seiyukai was too highly trained to rush in. Now, suspecting that he might be facing another ninja, he pulled back to reappraise the situation. In contrast, Gama was too close to the Ninja Master to escape. He did not even have time to raise the *badik*. McKenna, turning slightly, caught him with a Gorju-Ryu karate lower upward kick, the instep of his right foot crashing into the Indian. Kesar Gama's body exploded with hurt, with an agony that was unbearable. Paralyzed with pain, he couldn't even scream. Only able to gasp and make strange gurgling noises, he let the *badik* slip from his hand and fell to his left side. Slobbering, quivering, he pulled his knees up to his chest.

In one quick movement, McKenna stooped, picked up the *badik*, and threw himself to the right to avoid Kakuzo Seiyukai, who had attempted a flying thunder kick. By the time the Dragon Claw Ninja had landed on both feet and had spun around, McKenna was facing him and saying in Japanese with a sneer, "With you, Inejiro Amida sent a little boy to do a man's job! You're so much of an amateur, you're not even fit to be a Hsueh T'u apprentice!"

Standing in a ready stance, Seiyukai hissed back in Japanese, "Who are you?"

"My name is Scott McKenna. I'm the man who is going to kill you!"